Charlie woke and she was spooned in a stranger's arms. Totally spooned.

She had her back to him, his arms were around her and her body was curved into his chest. His face was against her hair. She could feel his breathing.

She could feel everything else.

He was wearing boxers.

He wasn't totally naked.

He might as well be.

Her nightgown was ancient and flimsy, and she could feel his body against her. His chest was bare. His arms, muscled, strong, were holding her tight. Bare arms against bare arms. Skin against skin.

She could see chinks of sunlight through the drapes. The storm was over.

She should tug away, out of this man's arms.

She'd wake him and he'd been so good...

It was more than that, though.

She really, really wanted to stay right where she was. For the moment the world had stopped. Here was peace. Here was sanctuary.

Here was...Bryn?

A man she'd known for what, twelve hours? Most of that had been spent sleeping. *Oh, for heaven's sake... Get up*, she told herself.

But she didn't. She lay there and let the insidious sweetness of the moment envelop her.

Dear Reader,

I do love a good Cinderella story, with a beautiful heroine fallen on hard times and a hero to die for. The story of Cinderella, though, has always seemed unfairly stacked against our heroine. All the hero has to do is fix a glass slipper on her foot and he's done.

I make my hero work a bit harder for his happy-ever-after.

I've therefore thrown a few extra obstacles in the way of Charlie and Bryn's happy ending. Tragic pasts, conniving relatives, adorable dogs of dubious parentage, a dotty but aristocratic mama... I had the best of fun making sure Lord Carlisle of Ballystone Hall had to work to win his heroine. I wish you just as much fun reading his story.

Marion

English Lord on Her Doorstep

Marion Lennox

—

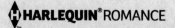

Recycling programs
for this product may
not exist in your area.

ISBN-13: 978-1-335-13527-8

English Lord on Her Doorstep

First North American publication 2018

Copyright © 2018 by Marion Lennox

Printed in U.S.A.

Marion Lennox has written more than a hundred romances and is published in over a hundred countries and thirty languages. Her multiple awards include the prestigious RITA® Award (twice), and the *RT Book Reviews* Career Achievement Award for "a body of work which makes us laugh and teaches us about love." Marion adores her family, her kayak, her dog and lying on the beach with a book someone else has written. Heaven!

Visit the Author Profile page
at Harlequin.com for more titles.

To Olga and Olga. With thanks for your friendship and your kindness, and for your generosity in finding my books so far away.

Praise for
Marion Lennox

"The story is one of a kind and very interesting. Once I started, I couldn't stop."

—*Goodreads* on *Stranded with the Secret Billionaire*

"This love story has a few unexpected twists and is even exciting at times. Lennox's imagination shines with her worldbuilding."

—*RT Book Reviews* on *His Cinderella Heiress*

CHAPTER ONE

BRYN THOMAS MORGAN, Twelfth Baron Carlisle, Peer of the Realm, thought his week couldn't get worse. It could.

It said a lot for his state of mind—weary, horrified and disgusted—that while he searched in the rain and the dark to find the dog he'd just hit, his head was already rescheduling.

If the dog was dead, he'd take it to the local police station, explain how he'd hit it on a blind curve and let the locals look after their own.

His plane back to London was leaving in three hours and he had a two-hour drive in front of him. He had time to scrape a dead dog from the road and catch his flight.

But when he finally found the soggy heap of fur that had been thrown into the undergrowth, the dog was alive.

Despite being hit by an Italian supercar?

Twenty years ago, when he was a boy learning to drive the estate's four-by-four across the vast estates of Ballystone Hall, his father had told him never to swerve for an animal. 'You'll lose control,' he'd told him. 'Animals can usually judge distance and speed. If you swerve, they're more likely to be hit, not less, and there's a possibility you'll kill yourself, too.'

But this hadn't been a farm-vehicle-savvy calf, darting back to the herd, or a startled but nimble deer. This dog was a trudger: a dirty white, mid-sized mutt. It had been square in the centre of the country road, head down, looking almost as if a car coming around the bend would be doing it a favour by hitting it.

So of course Bryn had swerved, but the road was rain-washed and narrow. There hadn't been time or space to avoid it. Now it lay on the grass at the roadside, its hind leg bloody, its brown eyes a pool of pain and misery.

Bryn stooped over it and those eyes were saying, 'Kill me now.'

'You didn't think of taking pills,' Bryn said, but he said it gently. He liked dogs. He missed them.

But the dogs at home were currently being cared for by his mother and by the farm staff who valued them as they deserved. Not like this one. This dog looked as if it had been doing it tough for a while.

What to do?

He was trying to beat a storm that threatened to close the country down for a couple of days. A line-up of lawyers was waiting to meet him in

London. He needed to get away from this mess and get back to Ballystone Hall, to the farm, to the cattle, to the work that filled his life. He also needed to finally accept the title he hated, and he still wasn't sure how to do that. The dreariness of the last months had hauled him close to the blackness he'd fought ever since...

No. Don't go there. Focus on getting on that flight.

But there was a dog. A bitch. Lying on the road. Bleeding.

It was a twenty-minute drive back to the last town. It was twenty-five minutes to the next.

It was eight o'clock at night.

The dog was looking at him as if she was expecting him to wield an axe.

'It's okay,' he told her, fondling the bedraggled ears. Forcing himself to think.

This was farming country, west of Melbourne. Where there were farms, there'd be a vet. He could ring ahead to warn he was coming, and pay whatever was needed to pass over the responsibility of taking care of her wounds and finding her owner.

But first he had to get her off the road. It was raining already and the distant rumbling of thunder threatened more.

The dog was bleeding. Blood was oozing rather

than spurting, but it was enough to be worrying. He needed towels.

He was travelling light and a towel wasn't included in the sparse gear he carried. He was in Australia to try and distance his name from his uncle's financial mess. The debt collection agency was due to collect this car from the airport's valet parking tomorrow. It'd be a great look if they found it smeared with blood, he thought. That'd add even more drama to the mess that was his uncle's life.

'A pill would definitely have been easier,' he muttered to the dog, but he was already shrugging off his jacket, figuring how to edge it underneath so he could carry her. Then he headed back to the car to find a spare shirt to wrap the leg.

'Okay, dog, hopefully it's only your leg that's damaged,' he told her as he worked. 'I'll ring ahead to the next town and have the vet meet me. Let's get you safe and warm before the eye of this storm hits. I might need to break the odd speed limit but I can still catch my plane.'

Charlotte Foster—Charlie except when she was with clients—didn't like storms, though maybe that was putting it too lightly. In her neat little interior-design studio back in Melbourne, with solid town houses on either side, she could pull the blinds, put something loud on the sound system and pretend storms didn't happen. Here, though, she was in a dilapidated farmhouse with a rusty tin roof, she had no neighbours for miles and she was surrounded by dogs who were already edgy.

If Grandma were here she'd sneak into bed with her. How many times had she done that as a little girl? This place had been her refuge, her time out. Grandma had scooped her up every school holidays and brought her back here, surrounding her with dogs, chaos, love.

She sniffed.

Charlie wasn't a sniffer but she'd been sniffing for weeks now, and sometimes even more than sniffing.

Grandma…

There was a hole in her heart a mile wide.

The dogs, too, were acting as if the bottom had dropped from their world, as indeed it had. In the weeks she'd been here Charlie still hadn't figured what to do with them. They were rejects, collected over the years by Betty who hadn't been able to say no to anyone. To anything.

Charlie still didn't know what would happen to them. There was no way she could take six dogs back to her studio-cum-bedsit—seven if you counted Flossie, although she'd almost given up on Flossie.

Betty's note was still haunting her. That last night…she must have felt it coming. Pain in her chest? Breathlessness? Who knew? Whatever, instead of doing the sensible thing and calling an ambulance straight away, she'd sat down and written instructions for Charlie.

You know most of this but just to remind you of details.

Possum is a sort of fox terrier. Nine years old. Loves his black and white sock more than anything. There are spares in my bottom drawer in case of disaster.

Fred's a part-basset, part-vacuum-cleaner. He'll eat anything on the basis he can bring it up later if it's not edible.

Don't let him near Possum's sock!

And so on.
But then, at the end…

Flossie's a sweetheart, but needy. You met her last time you came. She's only been with me for two months, dumped on the road near here. I need to keep her secure because any chance she gets she's off down the road, trying to find the low life who abandoned her.

Charlie had spent the last weeks caring for the dogs and other animals. Trying to figure a solution to the financial mess. Wanting to kill the

scumbag who'd fleeced her grandma. Trying
to block out the memory of her own stupidity,
which meant she had no resources to help now.
Her grief for the gentle Betty had been a constant
ache throughout, but adding to it was the fact that
when Betty had finally called the ambulance, the
paramedics had left the gate open.

Somewhere out there was a lost dog called
Flossie.

Charlie had enough on her plate with six dogs
she needed to rehome. Flossie surely must be
someone else's problem by now, but, still, she'd
searched. She'd hoped. Betty would expect her
to. Now, as the storm closed in, the thought of a
lost Flossie was breaking her heart.

'You guys can all come into bed with me until
it's over,' she told the dogs, who were getting
more nervous as the sound of thunder increased.

Flossie… She'd be out there somewhere…

'I've looked,' she said out loud, defiantly, to
a grandma who could no longer hear. To Betty,
who she'd buried with grief and with love ten days
ago. 'I've done all I can, Grandma. Now it's time
for me to bury my head under my pillows and get
through this storm without you.'

Yallinghup was the town ahead. It had a vet who
was currently somewhere in a paddock with a cow
in labour. He could hear the sound of wind in the

background when she answered the phone. 'I can meet you in an hour or so,' she'd said brusquely. 'Probably. Depends when this lady delivers. I'll ring you back when we're done.'

Carlsbrook was the town behind. 'Dr Sanders is on leave,' the not so helpful message bank told him. 'In case of emergency please ring the veterinarian at Yallinghup.'

The dog was now lying on his passenger seat, looking up at him with huge, scared eyes.

Okay, next step…or maybe it should have been the first step. Find the owner. However, this wasn't exactly suburbia, with lots of houses to door-knock. This was farming country, with houses set back behind towering gum trees. He couldn't remember passing a house for the last couple of miles.

'But you must have come from somewhere,' he told the dog and fondled her ears again while he located her collar.

Flossie.

No more information. Great.

'Okay, next farmhouse,' he muttered and hit the ignition. 'Please let it be your owner, or at least someone who'll understand that I need to be gone.'

She really, really didn't like storms. She didn't like the dark.

She didn't like anything about this.

She should feel at home. She'd been coming here since she was a little girl, every school holidays, and she'd loved being here, helping Betty with the dogs, the chooks, the myriad animals Betty had housed and cared for.

She loved this place, but it was love of Betty that made her keep visiting, and it was that love that was making her stay now.

Three weeks ago Charlie had been finally starting to get over the mess her own life had become. She'd been scraping a living as an interior designer. That living had depended on her being at her studio to receive clients, but she couldn't be there now—because of Betty.

And Betty would never be here again. That was enough to make her feel desolate, even without thunderstorms. Now… There'd been five huge claps of thunder already and the rain was turning to a torrent, smashing against the tin roof so loudly it made her shudder. She needed to bolt for the bedroom and hunker down with the dogs.

But then…

Someone was knocking at the front door.

What the…?

Normally a knock at the front door would have meant an explosion of canine excitement but there was no excitement now. Charlie was in the farmhouse kitchen, and the dogs were lined up behind her, as if Charlie were all that stood between them and the end of the world.

Or the stranger at the door?

For there was someone there. What she'd assumed was lightning must have been car lights sweeping up the drive.

Who? Every local knew that Betty was dead. The funeral had seen almost the entire district turn out, but since then she'd been left alone. It was assumed she was here to put the place on the market and move back to the city.

She wasn't one of them.

So now... It was dark. It was scary.

Someone was knocking.

Weren't dogs supposed to protect?

'You guys come with me,' she muttered and grabbed Caesar and Dottie by the collars. Caesar was mostly wolfhound. Dottie was mostly Dalmatian. They were both cowards but at least they were big, and surely that had to count for something?

She hauled them into the hall. The knocker sounded again over the rumble of more thunder.

She had a dog in each hand. Four more dogs were supposed to be lined up behind her. Or not. Three had retreated to the living room. She could see three tails sticking out from under the ancient settee. Only Mothball remained. Mothball was a Maltese-shih-tzu-something, a ball of white fluff, not much bigger than Charlie's hand, but what she lacked in size she made up for in heroics. She was bouncing around Caesar and Dottie as if to say, I'm here, too, guys. But Caesar and Dottie were straining back, wanting to add their tails to the settee pack.

Nothing doing.

'Who's there?' Charlie managed, thinking as she said it, Is an axe murderer going to identify himself?

'My name's Bryn Morgan.' The voice was deep, imperative, sure. 'I'm hoping you might be able to help me. I have an injured dog here and I hope you can tell me where I might find the owner. The name tag says Flossie.'

Flossie? She let her breath out in one long rush. Flossie!

'Please,' she said out loud, a prayer to herself, to Grandma, to anyone who might listen, and she opened the door to hope.

The house was two storeys of ramshackle. The veranda was wide and wobbly. Floorboards had creaked and sagged as he'd crossed it, and the line-up of saggy, baggy settees along its length added to its impression of something straight out of Ma and Pa Kettle. Or maybe the Addams family, Bryn thought ruefully, as a sheet of lightning seared the sky before he was plunged into darkness again.

And then the door opened.

Light flooded from the hallway within. Dogs surged forward, though not lunging, simply heading for a sniff and welcome—though there was a warning yip by an ankle-sized fluffball.

And behind them was a woman. Youngish. Late twenties? She was short, five feet four or so, with bright copper curls tumbling around a face devoid of make-up. She looked a bit pale. Her eyes were wide…frightened? She was wearing faded jeans and a huge crimson sweater. Bare feet.

She was looking straight past him.

'Flossie,' she said and her voice held all the hope in the world.

Thank you, he breathed to whoever it was who was looking after stranded and stressed gentry in this back-of-beyond place. To have lucked on the owner… He could hand her over and leave.

'You have Flossie?' she demanded, her voice choking. 'Where?'

'She's in my car,' he said, apologetically. 'I'm so sorry but I've hit her.'

'You've hit…' He heard the catch of dread. 'She's not dead?'

'She's not dead.' He said it strongly, needing to wipe that look of fear from her face. 'She's hurt her leg but I can't see any other injuries and her breathing seems okay. I'm hoping the wheel skimmed her leg and nothing else was injured. But the vet—'

'That's Hannah Tindall. Yallinghup. I have her number.' She was already reaching for the phone in her back pocket. 'I'll take her straight—'

'Hannah's delivering a calf,' he told her. 'She should be through in about an hour. The vet at Carlsbrook's on leave.'

'You've already rung?' She took a breath and then another. 'Thank you. I…is she in your car?' She stepped towards him, past him, heading into the rain.

He was wet. She wasn't, and Flossie had already shown she was amenable to him carrying her. There was no reason for both of them to get soaked. He moved to block her.

'Find some towels,' he told her, gently now as if he was treating two shocked creatures instead of one. As maybe he was. 'Do you have a fire? She's wet and I think she needs to be warm.'

'I…yes. The kitchen… I have the range on…'

'Go grab towels and I'll bring her in,' he said and then hesitated. 'That is, if it's okay?' He looked past her into the hall. 'Do you have anyone to help?'

'I…' She took another deep breath and visibly regrouped. 'No, but it's okay. Of course it is.

Please bring her in. Thank you so much.' Her voice broke a little. 'Oh, Flossie…'

She disappeared, almost running, into the back of the house, leaving the door wide and Bryn thought…what had he just asked her to do?

He wasn't thinking. The chaos of the last weeks had pretty much robbed him of logical thought.

He shouldn't have asked for access to the home of a solitary woman late at night. She'd run for towels and left him in the doorway, with total trust.

Trust. There was a word that had been lacking in his life for the last weeks. The days of interrogation, the sick sensation in his gut as he'd realised the extent of his uncle's dishonesty, the appalling feeling as he'd checked the local media…they'd made him feel as if he were smeared with the same smutty tar brush as his uncle. Yet here he was, in this woman's home, totally trusted. He should go give her a talk on trust and where it could lead—but she was trusting for a reason and he needed to honour it.

He headed back into the rain, which seemed to be increasing in intensity by the moment, gathered one injured pooch carefully in his arms and carried her inside.

The dog seemed limp, listless. Her bones were sticking out of her ribcage. If the woman hadn't been surrounded by visibly well-cared-for dogs he'd have suspected neglect but there was no neglect here. As he walked back into the hall she reappeared with her arms full of towels. She dropped them as she saw the dog in his arms—and burst into tears.

'Oh, Flossie…' She was sensible though, he thought. She didn't rush to hug. She came close and touched the dog behind her ear, a feather-touch. 'We thought we'd lost you. Oh, Grandma…' And then she hauled herself together, stooped and gathered the towels again and led the way into the kitchen.

It was a great kitchen. A farmhouse kitchen in the very best sense of the words. It was cosy and faded, with worn linoleum, an ancient wooden table and random wooden chairs with cheerful, non-matching cushions tied to each with frayed gingham bows. An ancient dresser took up almost the length of one wall and the opposite wall held the range and an extra electric oven—presumably for days when it was too hot to light the fire. The range was lit now, its gentle heat a welcome all on its own. A tatty, faded rug stood before the range and an ancient settee stood to one side. There were photographs stuck randomly to the remaining wall space, dogs, dogs and more dogs, plus the odd faded family shot. A guy in khaki took pride of place in the photograph display but the dog pictures were edging in, overlapping, as if the soldier's memory was being gradually over-laid by woofers.

Something was simmering on the stove. Something meaty and herby.

The whole effect was so comforting, so far from the bleakness of the last few days—so reminiscent of home?—he stopped dead in the doorway and had to take a moment to take it in. Which was used to good effect as the woman darted forward and hauled the settee closer to the fire.

'Put her down here. Oh, Flossie…'

And Flossie gave an almost imperceptible wiggle of her tail, as if she too recognised the kitchen for what it was. A sanctuary, a place almost out of this world. A time capsule where everything in it seemed safe.

He caught himself. Dog. Settee. He walked forward and settled her with care on the towels the woman laid out. Flossie's tail wagged again as her body felt the comfort of the settee and she looked adoringly up at the woman hovering beside her.

'Oh, Flossie…' the woman murmured again. 'What have you done to yourself?'

'I can't see anything obvious apart from the leg,' Bryn told her. 'I'm not sure if it's broken or not.' It was badly grazed, still sluggishly bleeding. 'I can't feel anything else but she hasn't moved.'

'It could be shock,' the girl said. 'And hunger. She's been missing for three weeks.'

'Three weeks!'

'I know.' She shook her head. Her fingers were running lightly over the dog's sides, watching for reaction. 'She's a stray, dumped here a couple of months back. People do that—toe-rags. They don't want an animal so they think, I know, we'll dump it outside a farm. And of course everyone knows Grandma takes strays in. So Flossie was dumped but she must still remember being thrown from the car. So off she went and I've looked so hard…'

The emotion he heard in her voice was for a stray dog she'd only known for weeks?

'That's your jacket underneath her,' she said, seeming to notice the soft leather for the first time. 'Oh, heavens, it'll be ruined. I'll get it out for you… I don't know… Can I give you something towards cleaning?' She paused and seemed to regroup. 'Sorry. I'm not thinking clearly.' She took a deep breath. 'I'm Charlie Foster, by the way. Charlotte. You're… Bryn Morgan, did you say? I'm very pleased to meet you and I'm deeply thankful for your help, but I can manage now. I'll ring the vet as soon as she's available. Once Flossie's cleaned and fed, though, I'm hoping I might not need her. You've done…great. Thank you so much.'

She moved to edge the jacket out but he stopped her. 'Leave it.'

'You don't want your jacket?'

Um…not. Carrying a blood-soaked jacket back to the UK…it was a good one but not that good. 'It's fine,' he told her. 'Are you sure you're all right here? Your grandmother…'

'I'm fine.' She straightened and reached out and took his hand, shaking it with a firmness that told him this was a woman of decision. 'You've been fabulous, Mr Morgan, but there's nothing more you can do. I won't keep you any more.'

Great. He could step away, head back to the car. He could even make it to the airport in time.

'You're sure you'll be okay?'

'I don't think there's anything more you can do.' Which wasn't quite answering the question, but he agreed with her. The dog's tail was wagging, feebly but with every indication that warmth and food and medical care to her leg would see her recover. There was nothing more he could do, and he had a plane to catch.

'I'll see myself out, then.'

'Thank you so much.'

The hand clasping his… It was a clasp of friendship and gratitude and it made him feel…

Like he hadn't felt for a very long time. Not since he'd left home.

Maybe not even then.

He looked down at her, at her tumbled curls, at her face, devoid of make-up, flushed now with the warmth of the fire, her brown eyes direct and clear. She was smiling at him. She was half a head shorter than he was.

She made him feel…

He didn't have time to feel. He had a plane to catch.

'Good luck,' he told her, and on impulse he grabbed a pen lying on the table and wrote his name and email address on a pad that was clearly used for shopping lists. 'Will you let me know how things go? And if there are any veterinarian bills… I hit her. I'm more than happy to cover them.'

Something flashed over her face that might have been relief but was quickly squashed. 'It's okay. It wasn't your fault.'

'But you will let me know.' He took her hand again. It seemed strangely imperative that he didn't release it until he had her agreement. To head off and not hear anything seemed the pits.

'I will let you know,' she said and tugged her hand away and that was that.

He turned and headed back out into the night.

Why had it been so hard to tug her hand back?

It was the dark, she told herself. Plus the storm. Plus the fact that she had an injured dog on her hands and she wasn't as sure of treating her as she'd told the guy… Bryn.

Anyone would want company on such a night, she told herself, but there was a blatant, very female part of her that told her that what she was feeling was more than that.

The guy was gorgeous. More than gorgeous. He was tall, clean-shaven, dark hair, a ripped and tanned body, wearing good chinos and a quality shirt open at the throat. His voice had been lovely, deep, gravelly, English, with just a hint of an accent that might have been…something? Welsh, maybe. That'd fit with his name. Bryn. Nice name.

He'd been carrying her beloved Flossie with tenderness. There was enough in all those things to make her think…hormonal stuff, and he'd looked at her with such concern… He'd smiled, a lopsided smile that said it was sensible to leave but he didn't like leaving her alone.

The smile behind those dark, deep-set eyes was enough to make a girl's toes curl.

But men who made Charlie's toes curl had no place in her life. She'd been down that road, and never again. Besides, a woman had other things to do than stand here and feel her toes curl. Bryn was heading out of her life, and she had an injured dog to attend to.

But life had other plans.

She turned back and stooped over Flossie just as a vast sheet of lightning made the windows flash with almost supernatural light. There was a fearful crash, thunder and lightning hitting almost simultaneously. And then…extending into the night…something more. A splintering crash of timber.

There was a moment's pause, and then something crashed down, so hard the house shook, and her feet trembled under her. Every light went out. The dogs came flying from wherever they'd been and huddled in a terrified mass around her legs. She knelt and gathered as many of them into her arms as she could.

It must be a tree, she told herself. One of the giant red gums in the driveway must have come down. And then she thought… Bryn. Dear God, Bryn… He was out in that. Almost before the thought hit, she was on her feet, shoving the dogs aside, heading through the darkness to the outside door…

And just as she reached it, it swung open.

'Charlie?'

Light was flickering through the doorway, lighting his silhouette. A tree on fire? She couldn't see enough to make out his features, but she could see his form and she could hear.

'Bryn…' She backed away, almost in fright, and the dogs gathered again around her legs. She stooped to hug them again, more to give herself time to recover than to comfort them. For what she really wanted was to hug the man in the doorway. For an awful moment she'd had visions of him…

Don't go there. The vision had been so appalling it still had her shaking.

'I'm very sorry,' he said and he sounded it. 'But there's now a tree across the driveway.'

'Are you okay?' Her voice wasn't working right. 'You're not hurt?'

'Not a scratch.' He said it surely, strongly, as if he realised how scared she must have been. 'But I appear to be stuck. Unless there's another road out? I'm so sorry.'

For heaven's sake… He'd brought her dog home. He'd almost been killed by one of the trees she'd told her grandmother over and over were too close to the house. And *he* was apologising?

'There's no way out while it's pouring,' she told him. 'I…the paddocks will be flooding. And those trees…red gums…they're sometimes called widow makers.'

She caught a decent sight of him as the next flash of lightning lit the sky. He was wet, she noticed. He must have been wet before this. She'd been too caught up with Flossie to notice anything except how…

Um…she wasn't going there.

In fact she was having trouble going anywhere. She was having trouble getting her thoughts to line up in any sort of order.

'Widow makers?' he queried, helpfully, and she struggled to pull herself together. She rose and faced him, or she faced the shadow of him. Every light was gone but the lightning was so continuous she could make him out.

'That's what they're called. The trees. River red gums. They're notorious. They drop branches, often on hot, windless days, when it's least expected. They look beautiful and shady and people camp under them.'

'Or park under them?'

'Yeah, and bang…'

'It's not exactly a hot, windless day.'

'No, but they're so tall they're the first thing that lightning strikes and Grandma won't… wouldn't…clear the ones near the house. Even the dead ones. She says they made nesting sites for parrots and possums. She says… She said…'

And then she stopped.

'Said,' Bryn said at last, very gently, and she flinched.

'I…yes. A heart attack, three weeks ago. That's why…that's why I'm here. These are Grandma's dogs.'

'So you are here alone.'

She shouldn't say it. It was really dark. He was nothing but a shadow in the doorway.

She should tell him she had a bevy of brawny men sleeping off a night at the pub upstairs.

She didn't.

'Yeah,' she said. 'And I'm not very good with storms.'

'Neither am I,' he told her. 'Do you have a lamp? Torches?'

'I...yes.' Of course she did. Or Grandma did. This was a solitary country house, with trees all around. Power outages were common, happening often when Charlie was visiting.

Not as scary as this one though.

She fumbled her way back into the kitchen, to the sideboard, and produced a kerosene lamp. It was older even than Grandma, she thought. Lit, though, it produced a satisfactory light.

Bryn hadn't followed her into the kitchen. He'd stopped at the door, a darkened, watchful shadow.

Her fingers trembled as she lit the wick and relaced the glass, and he saw.

'Charlie, I'm safe as houses,' he said gently. He thought about that for a moment and then he smiled, finally coming further into the room to inspect her handiwork. His voice gentled still further. 'I am safe,' he repeated. 'In fact, I'm even safer than houses that have red gums all around them. You think anything's likely to crash down on our heads? You think we should evacuate?'

She adjusted the wick until it stopped smoking, then turned back to the sideboard to find more.

Grandma had half a dozen of these beauties, filled and ready to go.

The good thing about that was that she didn't have to look up. She could play with the lamps on the sideboard. She could speak without looking at him, which seemed…important. 'It seems…more dangerous to leave,' she managed. 'Even if there was a way out. And they say lightning doesn't strike twice in the same place.'

'There seem to be a lot of trees,' he said doubtfully. 'Do you think *same place* includes every tree less than twenty feet from the house?'

Oh, for heaven's sake… She swung around and glared. 'Mr Morgan, it seems…it seems you're stuck here for the night. I'm very grateful, and I'm not scared of you. But I am scared of storms. So while I'm happy to give you a bed for the night, supper, a place by the fire, it's predicated on you manning up and saying things like, "She'll be right," and, "What's a little lightning?" and, I don't know, "Singing in the rain" kind of stuff. So if you dare tell me there's a snowball's chance in a bushfire that another tree will come down and squash me, then you can step right out in the rain and take your chances. So what's it to be?' And she put her hands on her hips, jutted her chin and fixed him with such a look…

It was a look that even made him chuckle.

And imperceptibly his mood lightened. His

night was messed up. More than his night. All he wanted was to be back at Ballystone, home with his dogs and his cattle, with this disaster behind him. He should be glowering himself.

Instead he found himself grinning at the redheaded firebrand in front of him, and searching for words to make him...what had she demanded? Man up?

'Don't take no notice of me, ma'am,' he drawled, still grinning, searching for a voice that might match the description. 'Yep, one of those tiddly little trees might fall but if it do, I'll be out there catching it with one hand and using it as kindling for your stove. You need more kindling? Maybe I could go out and haul in that tiddler that just fell.'

Their eyes locked. Her defiance gave way. A dimple appeared, right by the corner of her mouth, and the laughter he'd tried for was reflected in her eyes.

'What if I say yes?' she ventured, a tiny chuckle preceding her words.

'Your wish is my command,' he said nobly and then looked out to where he could see the ruins of the vast tree smouldering and sparking across the driveway. 'I might need a pair of heatproof gloves, though. That tree looks hot.'

And gloriously, she gave a full-on chuckle. It was a good laugh, an excellent laugh, and it produced a flash of insight. Looking at her, at the signs of strain around her eyes, at her pale face, he thought it'd been a while since this woman laughed.

It felt good...no, it felt excellent that he'd been able to make it happen.

'You want help with Flossie?' he asked, bringing reality back into the room, but the smile stayed behind her eyes as she answered.

'Yes, please. I would. Do you know much about dogs?'

'I've had dogs all my life.' He hesitated, still trying to keep that smile on her face. 'But is it manly to confess I faint at the sight of blood?'

'You carried her in. There's blood on your shirt.' It was an accusation.

'So I did,' he said, sounding astounded. 'And so there is, and I haven't fainted at all. Let's try this new world order out, then, shall we? Let's get your Flossie bandaged before my manliness fades before my very eyes. Okay, Nurse, I require more light, hot water, soap, um...'

'Bandages?'

'Of course, bandages,' he said and grinned and then looked down at Flossie, waiting patiently before the stove. 'And do you have a little dog food? A water bowl? I don't know how long it is since she's eaten but I'm guessing that may be the first priority.'

It was the first priority. She headed for the fridge to find some meat but her head wasn't entirely focussed on the first priority.

This man behind her was…beautiful.

CHAPTER TWO

ON CLOSE EXAMINATION Bryn decided Flossie's leg was probably not broken. She'd lost a lot of fur. An abrasion ran the full length from hip to paw but she was passive as Bryn cleaned, and when he tentatively tested the joint she barely whimpered.

She did, though, react with extraordinary speed when Charlie produced a little chopped chicken. And then a little more. She wolfed it down and lay back, limp again, but with her eyes fixed adoringly on Charlie. Her one true love.

'That's hardly fair,' Bryn objected. 'I get the messy part and you get the kudos.' He snipped off the bandage he'd been winding and looked at dog and girl. Charlie's nose was almost touching Flossie's. Her curls were tumbling over the dog's head. Flossie looked as if she hadn't seen a bath for months but Charlie seemed oblivious. Germs obviously weren't worthy of a mention.

'She could do with a wash,' he said and Charlie looked at him with the scorn he obviously deserved.

'You're suggesting we undo that nice white

bandage, take her away from the fire and dump her in a tub.'

Flossie was looking at him, too, and the reproach in both their eyes…

Once again he had that urge to chuckle. Which felt good. Bryn Morgan hadn't chuckled in a long time.

He rubbed Flossie behind the ears. With the thunderstorm receding to a distant rumble, the complete doggy tribe was in the kitchen, nosing around with interest. A couple edged in for an ear-rub as well and suddenly he had a line-up.

'You can't pat one without patting all of them,' Charlie said serenely and once again he heard that chuckle.

It was a gorgeous chuckle. It made him…

Um, not. He had enough complications on his plate without going there. What was in front of him now?

He was sitting on faded kitchen linoleum before an ancient range, vintage kerosene lamps throwing out inefficient light but enough to show the raggle-taggle line-up of misbegotten mutts waiting to have their ears rubbed. While a woman watched on and smiled. While outside…

Um…outside. You could buy a house for the price of the car he'd been driving. How was he going to explain that one?

'I have a good, thick soup on the stove,' Charlie said, interrupting thoughts of irate bankruptcy trustees and debt collectors and car salesmen who still hardly believed in his innocence.

He focussed on the dogs instead. Would there be jealousy if he spent say one and a half minutes on Dog One and then two on Dog Two? He decided not to risk it and checked his watch. Charlie noticed and smiled.

'Do you have overnight gear in the car?' she asked. 'I could lend you an umbrella.'

That hauled him back to the practical. Overnight. Of course. He was genuinely stuck here. There were all sorts of problems he should be facing rather than how many seconds he'd been rubbing Dog One.

One of those was where his overnight gear was right now.

'You have a spare bed?' he asked, cautiously.

'I do. I'll put you at the back of the house to give you a little peace because the dogs sleep with me. Except Possum. She usually sleeps by the back door. She's my guard dog but if there's any more lightning she'll be in with me. And Flossie will definitely be with me.'

'You'll sleep with Flossie?' She really was filthy.

'I'm sure it's good, clean dirt,' she said cheerfully. 'And I can't tell you how much I've worried about her. If I had half a kingdom I'd hand it to you right now.'

'Do you have a spare toothbrush instead?'

She blinked. 'Pardon?'

'I'm a bit averse to lightning,' he confessed. 'I'm happy for my overnight gear to stay where it is.' Wherever that was. Under one enormous tree.

He should tell her, he thought, but she was pale enough already and the knowledge that he'd been two seconds from climbing into the car and being pancaked was something she didn't need to hear about tonight.

He didn't want to think about it tonight.

'I do have a spare toothbrush,' she told him. 'I was at a conference in a gorgeous hotel…some time ago…' In another life. Moving on… 'The free toothbrush was so beautifully packaged I stuck it in my toilet bag. If you don't mind pink sparkle, it's yours.

'You'd give up pink sparkle for me?'

'I said you deserve half my kingdom,' she said and she was suddenly solemn. 'I mean it.'

'Then let's go with one toothbrush, one bowl of soup and a bed for the night,' he told her. 'I'll ask for nothing more.'

'Excellent,' she said and shifted across to help with the ear scratching. 'Soup and toothbrush and I don't know about you but I'm thinking bed's next on the agenda.'

Her arm brushed his and with the touch…
Things changed.

The tension was suddenly almost palpable.
Were both of them thinking the same?

'In your dreams,' she said, sounding breathless.

Of all the stupid… Were the tensions between
them so obvious? And she caught it. 'I didn't
mean…you know I didn't mean…' she stammered.

'I wasn't thinking,' he said, blankly, but he was
lying.

'Yes, you were.'

'If I was, I shouldn't have.'

'I know nothing about you,' she said and then
caught herself. 'But even if I did…'

'I'm a farmer from the UK,' he told her, feeling
a sudden urge to explain himself. Get things on a
solid basis. 'Thirty-five years old, here on family
business. I'm heading back to London tomorrow.'

'It still doesn't mean I'm going to bed with you.'

'Of course it doesn't.' He managed a lopsided
smile. What was it about the night that was making things so off kilter? 'Maybe electrical storms
act like oysters,' he tried. 'But we're grown-ups
now. We can handle it.'

'Yeah,' she said but sounded doubtful.

'So let's do introductions only,' he said, trying
to sound firm. 'We'll get this on a solid basis.
Not as a preamble to anything else. Just to clear
the air.' More, he didn't want to make it compli-

cated. Keep it simple, he told himself, and did. 'I've said I'm a farmer. I live a couple of miles from the Welsh border and I've been out here because my uncle's…'

That brought him up. How to explain Thomas? He couldn't. Not tonight. Hopefully not ever. He didn't even want to think of Thomas. 'My uncle's been living locally for a while,' he said at last. 'He's moved on, but I needed to deal with things he left behind. But it's done now. What about you?'

She looked at him doubtfully, as if she wasn't sure who he was and what on earth was happening. Which was pretty much how he was feeling. Tensions were zinging back and forth that had nothing to do with the lightning outside. Or maybe they did. Electricity did all sorts of weird things.

Like make him want…

Or not.

'I'm an interior designer,' she said at last. 'I had… I have my own business in Melbourne. But right now I'm babysitting seven dogs, two cows and fifteen chooks, trying to find them homes. Waiting for a miracle, which is not going to happen. Meanwhile, Mr Morgan, I have things to do, and not a single one of them involves thinking inappropriate thoughts about anyone, much less you. So you get these ears scratched and I'll get the soup on and we'll go from there.'

'And I'll be gone in the morning.'

'Of course you will,' she said briskly. 'Just as soon as I...' And then she faltered. 'I'm sorry. The tree...it'll take money to get that cleared.' But then her face cleared. 'It's okay though. As long as your car has decent clearance and the paddocks don't flood too badly, we can cut through a few strands of fencing and get you out across the paddocks.'

Decent clearance...right.

'We'll worry about it in the morning,' he said and she sighed.

'That's my mantra.' She rose stiffly to her feet and looked down at him in the dim light. 'That's what I tell myself every night...worry about it in the morning. Wouldn't it be wonderful if I didn't have to?'

The first storm front passed. The wind and thunder and lightning eased. Bryn slept solidly, in a decent bed, a hundred times better than the hard-as-nails motel bed he'd stayed in for the last few days. Carlsbrook was a one-pub, one-general-store town and why his uncle had set up base there...

But he knew why. Carlsbrook was a far cry from the resort-style lifestyle his uncle favoured but it was a district of smallholdings, of farmers proud of their cattle. It also had an aging population and sparse and difficult Internet connection, a district often cut off from the outside world.

It was a population ripe for his uncle's scumbag activities.

But tonight he hardly thought about his uncle. He slept deeply, in an ancient four-poster bed on the second floor, while the wind whirled around the ancient weatherboards and trees creaked and groaned. There was something about this house, this home… The dogs.

This woman…

It felt like home. It was a strange sensation. Home was a long way away, Ballystone Hall, hard on the Welsh border. It was a magnificent place to live, but he never slept well there. But here, in this bed with its tatty furnishings, he fell into a sleep that was almost dreamless.

He woke as the second storm front hit.

It hit with such force he felt the whole house shudder. The thunderclap was so loud, so long, that the shuddering was more than momentary, and the lightning that flashed across the sky made a mockery of the window drapes. It lit the whole house with an eerie light.

The second clap of thunder followed the first, even louder, even stronger.

And two seconds later a dog landed on his bed.

A second after that, five dogs followed.

He'd assumed they were sleeping with Charlie.

They'd definitely abandoned ship though, or abandoned their mistress. The first one in, Stretch, was a sort of dachshund with a whiskery beard that said something had happened to impede an ancient pedigree lineage. He launched himself up onto the bed, and before Bryn could stop him he had his nose under the sheets, wriggling under the covers and heading down to Bryn's toes.

The next five dogs were all for following suit, but by then Bryn was prepared and had the sheet up to his neck.

And then the next lightning sheet lit the room and he looked at the door and Charlie was standing in the doorway holding a lamp. She was wearing a faded lacy nightgown and bare feet. Her hair was tousled as if she'd had a restless sleep. Her eyes were huge in her face and in her arms she carried Flossie. Whose eyes were also huge.

'I… I've been deserted,' she whispered. 'The dogs are scared.'

'And so are you?' He was trying not to smile. Dogs, woman, the whole situation… And a woman in a wispy nightgown with a lamp. But she did look truly scared.

'If it hits the house…'

'Have you seen the size of those trees outside? It'll hit those first.'

Maybe that was the wrong thing to say. Her

face bleached even whiter. 'And the trees will hit the house.'

'Not on this side,' he said, struggling to think of the layout of the yard outside. His room backed onto the service yard out the back. The red gums were mostly at the front and the house was big. 'But it's really unlikely. I think the biggest has already been hit.'

'My bedroom's at the front.'

She stood there, her arms full of dog, and her face…

'Tell you what,' he said nobly. 'How about you sleep in here and I go sleep in your room?'

'N…no.'

'Charlie…'

'I don't like thunderstorms,' she whispered and there was an understatement. It was a big enough call that it had him throwing back the covers—shoving dogs aside in the process—and heading for the doorway. Heading for Charlie.

And when he got there, as soon as she was close, he realised the fear wasn't just on her face. She was trembling all over. The dog in her arms was trembling, too, and he realised why the dogs had abandoned Charlie en masse. They wanted a leader who wasn't terrified, and Charlie's face said she wanted exactly the same.

A pack leader. He could do this. It was kind of compulsory—that he moved to reassure. That he took the final steps and took her firmly into his arms.

And held.

Flossie was in there somewhere, sandwich squeezed, totally limp, totally passive. Bryn was wearing boxers and boxers only because his pjs were somewhere under a burning red gum. As he felt Flossie's rough coat against his bare skin he felt the dog trembling.

As Charlie was trembling.

He had Charlie around the waist. Her head was tucked into the crook of his neck as if she wanted to be close, closer.

He held her tight. His fingers splayed the width of her waist and his chin rested on her hair and he just…held.

And the feeling of home deepened, strengthened and something was happening…

Her hair was so thick, so soft, and it smelled of something citrusy, something gorgeous…

No, gorgeous was the adjective for the whole woman. For all of Charlie. That he be allowed to hold her…

She was totally still in his hold, yet not passive. She wanted to be held by him. There was a dog between them but he knew she wanted to be as close to him as she possibly could be.

Because she was scared. For no other reason.

This was a frightened woman and he was comforting her.

But she was gorgeous.

There was that word again. It was as if the word itself had seeped into his head and was changing something inside him.

Gorgeous.

Another clap of thunder shook the house and he felt her flinch. If it was possible, dog and woman clung tighter.

From back in the bed there were six terrified whimpers.

What was a man to do?

'Come to bed, sweetheart,' he murmured into her hair. 'You and me and seven dogs. We'll ride out this mother of a storm together.'

'Together...' He felt the war within, the fear of the storm, the fear of the stranger.

'We can do this,' he said. 'One bed, one man and one woman might be a problem. One bed, one man and one woman and seven dogs... I doubt there's a problem at all.'

She slept and there were seven dogs between her body and his. There was one clap of thunder too much, though, and at some time in the night, even in her sleep, her primeval fears must have overridden every other consideration. She woke and she was spooned in a stranger's arms. Totally spooned. She had her back to him, his arms were around her and her body was curved into his chest. His face was against her hair. She could feel his breathing.

She could feel everything else.

He was wearing boxers.

He wasn't totally naked.

He might as well be.

Her nightgown was ancient lawn and flimsy, and she could feel his body against her. His chest was bare. His arms, muscled, strong, were holding her tight. Bare arms against bare arms. Skin against skin.

She could see chinks of sunlight through the drapes. Flossie was lying at the end of the bed—she could feel her warm, welcome heaviness across her feet—but the rest of the pack had obviously taken off to check out the day. The storm was over.

She should tug away, out of this man's arms.

She'd wake him and he'd been so good…

It was more than that, though.

She really, really wanted to stay right where she was. For the moment the world had stopped. Here was peace. Here was sanctuary.

Here was… Bryn?

A man she'd known for what, twelve hours? Most of that had been spent sleeping. Oh, for heaven's sake… Get up, she told herself. Check on Flossie's leg. Go face the damage of the day.

But she didn't. She lay and let the insidious sweetness of the moment envelop her. She could lie here and imagine there were no problems. That Grandma wasn't dead. That she didn't have debts to her ears. That she didn't have to worry that she had no clue how to rehouse misfit dogs that she couldn't keep.

That she hadn't been betrayed by a low life herself, and that there seemed no one in the world who she could trust?

'Nice,' he murmured into her ear. 'You think if we stay here for long enough the rest of the world will disappear?'

So he was awake. And he had problems in his life, too? Well, didn't everyone? That made him… more human still.

Nice? No. Nice didn't begin to cut it. His body…if she didn't move soon…

And he got it almost the moment she did. 'Charlie, if we don't part I may well not be responsible for my actions,' he said and there was all the regret in the world in his voice. But she felt his body stir—where she most definitely didn't want his body to stir—and the fantasy had to end. As if in agreement, Flossie wriggled at the end of the bed and the day had to begin.

His arms released her. He shifted back. She

struggled to sit up and it felt like the greatest grief…

Which was ridiculous. Her body was responding to the heightened emotions of the last weeks, she told herself. It had nothing to do with the body of the man pushing back the covers and rising to his feet…

Dear heaven, he was breath-taking.

Last night he'd said he was a farmer and his body confirmed it. He looked weathered, tanned, ripped, as if he spent his life heaving hay bales or shearing sheep or hauling cattle out of bogs or… whatever farmers did.

Which reminded her…

'There's probably stuff to do,' he said as if he'd read her thoughts. 'Dogs to let out? To feed? Other animals?'

'Cows to attend,' she told him. 'And chooks to feed. That is, if they've survived the night. But there's no need for you to stay. If the ground isn't too wet you can run your car over the back paddock. I can cut the wire and let you out to the road.'

'And leave you on your own to cope with the mess?'

'It's my mess. I've kept you long enough. Where were you headed last night? Melbourne?'

'I was,' he said, ruefully, reaching for his trousers. It was such a domestic thing to do. She was lying in bed while the man beside the bed was dressing. It was discombobulating. Weird. 'I was heading for the airport.'

'Then you've missed your plane?' She sat bolt upright and stared at him in horror. 'Because of Flossie? Oh, no.'

'There'll be other planes.'

'Will you forfeit your ticket? I can… I'll…' Yeah, right, pay for another airline ticket? With what?

'Charlie…' He must have heard the panic in her voice because he leaned over and put his hands on her shoulders. It was a gesture that was meant to steady her, ground her, and in some ways it did. In other ways she felt not the least bit grounded. What the feel of this man did to her… 'I hit your dog,' he said, softly but firmly. 'This is my responsibility.'

'Flossie should never have been out on the road.'

'How did she get out?' He flicked a glance down at Flossie, who was curled against Charlie's legs as if she never wanted to leave. Maybe he could see her point.

'When Grandma had the heart attack the paramedics left the gate open and Flossie disappeared. That was three weeks ago. I have no idea where she's been since then. I've hunted everywhere.'

'You weren't here when your grandmother died?'

'I was in Melbourne. I did make it to the hospital before she died. She wanted to know about all the animals. I told her they were fine. I told her... I'd look after them.'

'So what's happening to them now?'

'I'm finding homes for them,' she said, with more certainty than she felt. 'I'm trying to fix the farm up so I can put it on the market...' Her voice faltered at that. It wouldn't be her putting it on the market, she thought. It'd be the bank, trying to scrape back anything it could. 'But now... your plane...'

'It doesn't matter. For now it seems we need to feed animals, feed us and then take a look at the damage outside.'

'You don't need to stay.' The thought of him missing the plane because of her... How could she ever make it up to him?

'You mean you're not offering me breakfast?'

'Don't you want to...just leave?'

'Without breakfast? That was great soup last night but it didn't cling to the sides. I saw your fridge last night. You have eggs. Bread. Mushrooms...'

'But your plane...'

'There'll be another plane tonight.' If there was a seat available.

'To London. You're English?'

'Part English, part Welsh.' He'd sat on the bed

and was pulling his boots on, and once more that impression of domesticity intensified. 'Where I live is border country.'

'Your farm…'

'My farm's in England. Just. Right, what's first? Will the dogs be downstairs waiting to be let out?'

'Grandma has a doggie door. She closed it when she had Flossie but since Flossie left…'

'I doubt if Flossie's thinking of leaving,' he said gently and leaned over Charlie to pat her.

And as if to deny his words Flossie struggled to her feet—well, three of her feet—and staggered across the bed towards him.

He scooped her into his arms and held her, smiling down at her.

'I'm thinking this girl's great,' he told Charlie. 'I suspect we don't even need the vet. But I also suspect there'll be a need for a nature call.'

'The yard outside the kitchen's enclosed,' Charlie told him. 'I'll be down in a moment. You won't let her out, will you?'

'I'll stay with her the whole time,' he said and then his smile turned to Charlie, a smile that almost had her heart doing back flips. Where did a man ever learn to smile like that?

'Take your time getting dressed, Charlie,' he said gently. 'I suspect you could do with a morning's break from responsibility. I'll check your charges and the damage outside.' He stooped and touched her face, a mere brush of finger against cheek. Why did that make her feel…as if she didn't know how she was feeling? 'You need help,' he told her. 'A morning might be all I can give, then I'll give it willingly.'

She took him at his word. She stood under the shower and tried to allow the hot water to calm her.

It sort of did. For some reason the appalling mess of the last weeks had receded. Someone was helping. What was more, she was trusting him. He was presently feeding the cows, collecting eggs and letting the hens out for the day, doing everything a farmer would know how to do.

But why was she trusting? How did she know who he was? Had the mess her grandmother had got herself into taught her nothing?

Oh, for heaven's sake, what was he going to do? Steal her eggs and run? There was little else left in the place to steal.

Everything was sold. All that was left was the valueless. A sad little cow and her bag-of-bones calf. Chooks that were almost past laying. Seven assorted dogs.

Her grandmother's jewellery box was empty. The shelves had long been stripped of anything saleable. Even the gorgeous old lounge suite, faded but beautiful, had been carted off to the auction rooms.

For the last few weeks Charlie had been consumed by an anger so deep, so vast it had threatened to overwhelm her. She hadn't been able to put it aside for a moment.

But now, with the hot water streaming over her naked body, her anger had been overlaid. She was suddenly thinking of a guy called Bryn with a lazy smile and gentle hands.

A man who'd held her in sleep.

A man who was getting on a plane tonight and she'd never see again.

Which was why she was getting out of the shower right now because standing under the hot water fantasising about the man was dangerous indeed—and besides, she was missing out on being…with him.

Or not. It was only because she needed to cook breakfast, she told herself as she tried to rub sense into herself with the threadbare towel. She had things to do. Sensible things.

She wasn't hurrying because Bryn was downstairs.

Liar.

Breakfast seemed top of the agenda but there was a problem. She came downstairs just as Bryn came through the kitchen door from outside, and she could read *problem* on his face.

'What?' she said with trepidation. 'Flossie…'

'Flossie's fine,' he said hurriedly. 'She's hopping on three legs but she lined up for her kibble with the rest of them. She even put a bit of pressure on her pad when she thought she was being beaten to the feed bowls.'

'You've fed them.'

'Yes, ma'am.' There was that smile again. 'I hope that's okay with you. I assumed that industrial drum of kibble by the back door was for them.'

'I'm not reduced to eating kibble myself,' she joked but it didn't come out as she'd meant it to. It came out sounding needy. But Bryn's smile had faded. He looked preoccupied. 'There's something else?'

'You have a cow in a bog,' he told her. 'The creek's a quagmire but she's obviously tried to reach it. I have no idea how she's worked herself into such a mess. Luckily her calf had the sense not to join her. The calf was standing on the bank making her displeasure at her mother's idiocy known to the world, but that's made things worse. The cow's desperate to reach her and has dug herself deeper. I've put the calf in the shed, so now we have one stuck cow to deal with. Do you have a tractor?'

'Um…no.'

'A neighbour with a tractor?'

She gazed out of the window at the debris scattered across the paddocks. Last night's storm had been appalling. Every local farmer would be out assessing damage to their own properties. Besides, Jock next door had been scathing of Grandma's cow and calf.

'Not even the knacker's 'll want them,' he'd told her when she'd tentatively asked if he could take them on. 'You can't take 'em back to your city apartment? The best thing to do is take 'em down to the back of the gully and shoot 'em. Tell you what,' he'd said in a spirit of neighbourliness because this was at Grandma's funeral and he was trying to be helpful. 'I'll do it for you if you like.'

She didn't like, and now…to ask if he'd abandon assessing damage on his place and spend the morning saving a cow…

Bryn was waiting for an answer. Did she have neighbours who'd help?

'No,' she said a bit too abruptly and got a sharp look in return.

'They're not helpful?'

'They'll be busy. And they don't think much of Cordelia.'

'Cordelia?'

'Cordelia,' she repeated. 'Her calf's Violet. And

don't ask. I have no idea how Grandma chose names.'

'Then I guess Cordelia needs to be dug out,' he said as if it was no big deal. He sounded almost cheerful. 'I might need some help. Can you show me where your spades are kept? And I'll need rope and planking...'

I might need some help...

See her gobsmacked.

Did he know how sweet those words sounded? For the last three weeks they'd been thrashing themselves around her head. *I might need some help...* She did need help. And now this man was assuming a bogged cow—*her* bogged cow—was his responsibility and he was asking for her help.

Did he know how close she was to bursting into tears on his chest?

Oh, my.

'But coffee first and toast,' he told her. 'She's in trouble but she's not going anywhere. If she was dumb enough to try and get to the creek to drink when all she had to do overnight was open her mouth and swallow, then she can wait until we fuel up. Toast and coffee and let's go.'

Charlie wasn't a farmer. Actually, neither was her grandmother. This place represented the remnants of the family farm, but Grandma had never been interested in farming. After her husband had died she'd sold off most of the land and committed herself to caring for injured wildlife. As she'd grown older she'd confined herself to dogs and chooks. Every now and then she'd let the neighbour bring his cows in to keep the grass down, but she'd spent the rest of her life collecting strays.

Six months ago she'd found a cow wandering along the road at dusk, a hazard to traffic, obviously neglected. Three weeks later it had given birth, much to Grandma's delight. Cow and calf were rangy, weird-looking bovines with no proven ancestry. No one had wanted them—except Grandma.

Charlie should have locked them in the sheds for the night. The truth was she didn't know how. How to make a cow go where it didn't want?

Bryn had, though. He'd driven the calf into the shed and Charlie was impressed.

Now they just had to deal with Cordelia.

Uh oh. Charlie walked down to the creek with Bryn and her heart sank.

Cordelia was obviously a cow accustomed to hard times. She'd sunk to her haunches in mud and was gazing down at the mire in deep despondency, as if thinking: If this is the way to go, then so be it.

'Grandma has troughs near the shed,' Charlie said as they gazed at the cow together. She was wearing jeans and wellingtons and carting a couple of spades. Bryn was wearing his gorgeous city shoes and the trousers and shirt he'd had on last night. He was carrying four lengths of planking and rope. She was trying not to be… aware of him. Very aware.

It wasn't working.

'I even left the shed door open,' Charlie told him indignantly, pushing aside inappropriate thoughts with difficulty. 'I went out in the rain especially but did she want to go in? No! And how do you get a cow to go where she doesn't want to go?'

'With a decent dog?' Bryn said and grinned down at the pack following them. They'd left Flossie sleeping by the stove, but the rest were bounding around them, joyous in the sunshine and the sense of doing. Cattle dogs? Not a one of them.

'You show me how and I'll train them,' Charlie told him.

He checked them for a moment, grin still in place. Possum, a sort of fox terrier. Fred, part basset, part…lots of things. Caesar, a wolfhound who trembled behind the back of the pack as if to say, Protect me, guys. Dottie, a Dalmatian so old her dots were faded to grey. Then there was Mothball, the fluffball, and Stretch, a sort of sausage dog whose tummy actually touched the ground when he ran. And Flossie back at the house.

'I can't imagine,' he said faintly.

'Don't you laugh at my dogs.'

'I wouldn't dare.' But still he grinned and she managed a smile back.

It really was a great morning. The sun was on her face. Her stomach was full of toast and coffee. She was still warmed with the memory of being held in this man's arms...

Whoa.

'Tell me where to dig,' she managed, a bit too fast, a bit...breathlessly.

'I'll do the digging.'

'You have to be kidding. In those clothes?'

'I already asked... You don't appear to have wellingtons in my size. Besides, that's what water's for. Washing.'

'Bryn...'

'What's the choice?' he asked.

And there wasn't one. Unless she went next door and borrowed a rifle.

No, there wasn't one.

'Right then,' Bryn said and laid down his planking and took the two spades from her shoulder. He laid one down on the ground. 'It's up to me.'

She picked it back up and glowered. 'It's up to us.'

'Right, ma'am,' he said and grinned again, looking ruefully down at his city shoes. 'You know, I should be bored out of my mind in a plane right now. How can I possibly regret my change of plan?'

It took skill, strength and patience to dig a cow out of a bog. Firstly there was the imperative of keeping the cow calm. Struggling would make her sink deeper and that was where Charlie came in.

'You've been feeding her for the last weeks?' Bryn asked and when she agreed he set her task.

'Right. You're the cow whisperer. You squat by her head, block as much of me as you can and tell her all about the hay bales back in the shed.'

'I want to dig.'

'We can't always get what we want,' Bryn said, unperturbed.

Charlie thought, Yeah, tell me about it.

So she stooped as ordered and tried to do the cow-whispering thing but the cow wasn't having a bar of it.

'It's as if she thinks we're trying to dig her out to turn her into sausages,' she said indignantly as Cordelia did a bit more thrashing and Bryn nodded.

'Some cows are bred for intelligence. Obviously not this one. Okay,' he conceded. 'Let's go for fast. Grab a spade and help.'

Excellent. She dug, ankle deep in mud, shovelling the squishy mud from in front of the cow.

'We need to get deep enough to lay planking

so she can haul herself up,' Bryn told her. 'But if you're getting blisters…'

'I'm not getting blisters.' She wasn't, but she was aware that as shovellers went she came a very poor second to the man beside her. He looked as if he'd shovelled a thousand cows out of bogs in his lifetime. His spade work was steady, methodical, effective, and he could load his shovel with twice as much sludge as she could.

He really was a farmer.

She was so lucky to have him here this morning. What good fairy had decreed he be the one to hit Flossie…and bring her home…and stay…?

Even hitting Flossie… Flossie must have been wandering for weeks. Sure, she'd been hit by a car, but this morning she was putting weight on her back leg, and if she still looked good when they got back to the house Charlie might not even have to pay for vet bills.

Magic.

Well, sort of magic. There were lots of things about her situation that weren't magic, but right now, steadily shovelling, she could put the worries of the world aside and soak in the moment.

Soak was right. Her gum boots weren't exactly effective. She was wet and filthy. And Bryn… Somewhere under the mud were his feet. They'd put the planks under their feet as they dug but it didn't help much. The mud was insidious.

He didn't appear to notice. A farmer born and bred.

'So your cows,' she said cautiously—she really would like to know more about him. 'Intelligent, are they?'

'You have to believe it,' he told her. 'Mensa candidates all.'

'Right.'

'You think I'm joking? My top ladies… I can call them by name.'

'How many ladies do you have?'

'Enough to keep me busy,' he said enigmatically and that smile returned again. 'More than you. It's hard to make a living with two cows. So how about you? Can you make a living interior designing from here?'

'No,' she said shortly. 'I need to get back to Melbourne. Just as soon as I find homes for all these guys.'

He paused and looked at Cordelia, who'd finally stopped struggling and now appeared to be bored. Then he glanced back at the assorted dog pack, gambolling in the sunshine. Misbegotten? Maybe that was too strong a word for it, but these dogs hadn't been chosen for their cute appeal.

'And what happens if you don't find them homes?' he asked, gently now because maybe he knew there were nerves he was touching.

'I have no idea,' she snapped. 'I can't see them

in a one-bedroom studio in Melbourne. Even if I could, I suspect my landlord would take a dim view.'

'Especially of Cordelia,' he agreed. 'Though we could wash her and spruce her up a bit. Maybe tie a few interior-design ribbons on her horns and set her up as a conversation piece.'

She didn't smile, she just kept on digging as the grey descended again. What were her options? They were down to practically zero.

Maybe it would have been a kindness to invite her neighbour over with his rifle.

'So tell me,' she said, desperate to change the subject. She was digging again, concentrating fiercely. 'Why are you in Australia? What put you on the road outside Grandma's place last night? I know you were heading for the plane but why were you here in the first place?'

'Family business.' That was curt. The smile had gone from his eyes.

'You said...your uncle? A death?' she queried, and she thought she shouldn't go there but anything to distract her from the thoughts of rifles and long-term outcomes.

'Not a death.' He paused in his digging. 'Let's shift these planks back a bit. I'm thinking if we take a bit out from where we are now we can slope the planks down to her. She could possibly struggle out now but she'd have nowhere to go.'

They messed around a bit, shifting planks, doing busy work while Bryn's face stayed grim.

There was stuff going on in this guy's life, too. Rifle kind of stuff?

'It's okay,' he said at last. 'No, it wasn't a death, though it could have been. My uncle's been in trouble. I've done all I can to help.'

'Financial trouble?'

'You could say that.'

'There aren't many farmers around here who aren't,' she said, sympathetically. 'The last drought—'

'He's not a farmer,' he said, curtly, cutting the conversation with a tone that said it was going no further. He had his planks adjusted and dug silently for a while. Charlie had paused. Not because her hands hurt, although her hands actually did hurt, but because Bryn was digging carefully now, forming a slope, and she needed to figure what was happening. He was making what was essentially a ramp.

And he didn't want to talk about his uncle.

Fair enough. It wasn't her business. And besides, they were getting to the pointy end of this rescue business.

Bryn stepped back and surveyed his handiwork. Cordelia looked up at them with bovine lack of interest, as if the ramp Bryn was making had nothing to do with her. Talk about dumb…

'Maybe she's cold,' he said, generously.

'Maybe she's thick,' Charlie responded. 'If I was her I'd see the ramp and be hauling myself up.'

'It's lucky she's not. She might sink again. Let's get these planks in position so she has something solid to grip.'

'And then you'll make her move how?'

'Pull,' he said solidly. 'One thing I've learned in thirty-five years of farm life is how to get dumb beasts to do what you need them to do. The only exception is my stupid uncle.'

And then there was silence as he roped the cow, as he checked the planks again, as he put Charlie at the far end of the rope and took a grip himself. It was seemingly a tug of war, with Cordelia on one team and Charlie and Bryn on the other.

But it felt okay, Charlie thought, as she gripped the rope in two hands and prepared to pull. For Bryn was behind her.

She was…a team.

'Count of three, pull,' Bryn ordered. 'One, two, three…'

And they pulled. Cordelia gave a vast, indignant bellow as if she'd decided she was quite comfortable in the mud and wouldn't mind staying there. But their grip was relentless, and finally she gave into the strain around her neck—and a leg squelched up from the mud and onto the planking.

'Harder,' Bryn said from behind her and she

gave one last heave—and Cordelia was up on the planks, heaving herself forward, then staring wildly towards the barn where the calf was bellowing. And two seconds later they were being shoved off the planks as a desperate, mud-coated cow was off and galloping towards her calf.

Charlie tumbled backwards. Bryn wheeled and caught her but overbalanced himself. Quick as lightning Bryn rolled sideways, lifting her high and rolling until she was off the mud and onto grass.

She was choking on laughter, lit with triumph. Bryn was holding her. The sun was on her face, but her face was coated with mud.

As was Bryn's. He was laughing, too, his dark eyes twinkling down at her. They were a muddy tumble of triumphant bodies and it seemed entirely appropriate that Bryn's arms stayed around her and held her, that laughter enveloped them, that Charlie twisted in his arms so she could see his face, so she could share his laughter.

And somehow, someway, for some ridiculous reason, it seemed entirely appropriate that Bryn should place his mud-smeared hands on either side of her mud-smeared face—and that he should kiss her.

A kiss… Here… Now… Of all the inappropriate things to do.

But it wasn't inappropriate.

Why?

Was this the culmination of weeks of shock, of grief, of stress, of hopelessness and, finally last night, of fear?

And sleeping in this man's arms?

Or was it simply wanting him?

For she wanted him and there was no doubting it. As her mouth met his, it was as if every nerve ending knew where it wanted to be centred and it was right here.

His kiss started tender, started as a question, but that question was answered with a definite yes. Her kiss back was the response he needed. The kiss turned strong, commanding, even possessive, and that was fine. No, it was more than fine, because right now she wanted to be...possessed? Maybe. For the last weeks she'd been spinning out of control, in some sort of crazy, non-predictable vortex. But right now her world had stilled, had centred, and it was centred on this man.

On this moment.

On the heat of his mouth.

She felt as if she were melting. The strength of him, the sureness...

He was a farmer and he felt like it, a man of the land, a man who knew how to get a frightened cow from a bog, a man who knew what a woman wanted.

She wanted him.

Which was crazy.

They were lying full length on the lush, storm-wet spring grass. The morning sun had little strength in it yet but she wasn't cold. Bryn was her heat source. He was her centre. He felt, he tasted, he held, like a man who could lift her out of the misery of the last few weeks.

In truth, he already had.

He was a stranger and he had a plane to catch back to England. This moment must be transient. But she was holding his face in her hands to deepen the kiss, holding as if she had the right to keep holding. She could forget everything else in the joy and the triumph of this moment—and who could blame her?

The kiss deepened and deepened again. If they'd been in the comfort of a bedroom instead of a soggy piece of turf, with water soaking fast through their clothes, then who knew what would have happened?

Or if Bryn hadn't had control because Charlie surely didn't…

But he did and, after a glorious few minutes of blocking out the world, the cold and wet finally permeated. Sense prevailed, and finally, reluctantly, they drew apart.

To laughter of course, because that was what this man seemed all about.

'Well,' he said. 'That was quite a morning. Is

that the way you always thank your farm hands
for services rendered?'

If they look—and feel—like you, she wanted
to say. But she didn't say anything. She couldn't.
She wanted this moment to stretch on for ever.

But Bryn was rising, holding out his hands,
tugging her up after him. She rose a little too fast,
so she was tugged close, breast against chest, and
when he put her back a little she wanted to protest.

But he was being sensible and so must she.

'We need to check Cordelia,' he said and there
was a reluctance in his voice that told her that
maybe he was feeling the same as she was. As if
the last thing she wanted was to move away from
this spot and check a muddy cow. 'We need to
let her into the shed to join her calf. And then we
need to dry off.'

Sensible. Right.

'I hope you have a change of clothes in the car,'
she said and was proud of how steady her voice
sounded.

'Cow first. We're not going to all that trouble
to have her die of hypothermia. Let's get her in
the shed with…what did you call her calf?'

'Violet.'

'Of course. How could I have forgotten Violet?'
He smiled down at her, and with the back of his
hand he traced a line down her muddy cheek. And
it was quite possibly the sexiest, most amazing

sensation she'd ever experienced. Every nerve in her body seemed to swerve, point, arrow itself to his touch. She wanted…she wanted…

Oh, for heaven's sake, she was a grown woman, and no matter what she wanted, she couldn't *have*. She had a cow to dry. Reality to face.

'Right,' she said, and with enormous difficulty she turned away and started trudging towards the outbuildings. Cordelia had already reached them and was bellowing her indignation at not being able to reach her calf. On the other side of the door Violet was bellowing in response. Charlie's problems slammed back.

What on earth could she do with two cows?

She was going to dry them, that was what, and then she'd do what came next, one step after another, for as long as she could. While this guy left and headed back to the UK. While the world turned as it always did, without noticing that one tiny speck seemed to have fallen off.

Now she was being melodramatic. She needed to get a grip. She squelched doggedly on but her foot landed on the edge of a wombat burrow and she slipped.

Bryn's hand came out and caught her and held, fast. And she let her hand stay.

Of course she did.

She needed to face reality—but not quite yet.

CHAPTER THREE

IT SEEMED BRYN knew exactly how to clean a filthy cow, which was just as well because Charlie had no clue. She'd have fussed about hot water—which wasn't exactly possible in a tumbledown barn, and Cordelia wasn't exactly small enough to take into the house and pop into the bath.

But Bryn simply hosed the worst of the mud from her—'Left on it'll cake and leave her cold.' And then found a bunch of rags. He handed some to Charlie and took more himself.

'We rub,' he told her. 'It'll warm us up as well as Cordelia. She is cold. We dry her, we feed her well and then we keep her in the shed with her calf until we're sure she's recovered. If we leave her like this she may well go down, and if she drops it'll be hard to get her up again. We've dodged one vet visit with Flossie. Let's not risk another.'

So despite her wanting to head into the house and a warm bath herself, she stood on the opposite side of a cow to Bryn and she rubbed and rubbed, and Bryn rubbed and rubbed…and it was more of the same, she thought. He…this whole situation…*this man*…made something happen to her body…to her mind?

Bryn's words kept playing in her head. *We. We* dry her. *We* feed her well.

We was a magical word. It made her feel shivery but not from cold.

How long since she'd been part of *we*?

The calf was nudging around them, heading for Cordelia's teats, backing out and checking them out and then darting under again. She was a strange-looking calf, still a bit bony from a malnourished start, but nosey and pushy and…fun? She had one huge white eye in an otherwise black face, which made her look like some sort of bovine pirate. She kept trying to shove Bryn out of the way as she tried to access her mother's teats and Bryn did his best to accommodate—but Violet was still pushy. She kept popping up from the teats to check on Charlie, and the sight of her pirate eye under Bryn's arm made Charlie want to chuckle.

Bryn was so good. His affection for the calf seemed immediate. He obviously loved animals.

The sight of him was doing something to Charlie that she didn't understand. Right now she didn't want to understand. She just wanted it not to end. She was still wet but the rubbing not only warmed her, but was somehow…mesmeric?

Bryn was talking in soothing tones to Cordelia. Cow talk? In Welsh?

'You're thinking she understands?' she asked.

'All cows know Welsh. It's international cow language.'

It was a very silly answer but she liked it. She went back to rubbing, insensibly happy at the ridiculousness of it.

'So why the trouble?' Bryn asked, gently, and it was like being pulled back into the real world but this was Bryn asking. He was leaving soon and somehow it didn't seem wrong that he should ask. But still, she didn't want to emerge from her happy place.

'Trouble?'

'I can see it on your face,' he said. The laughter had gone, but the gentleness remained. 'Trouble apart from your grandma's death.'

'I…'

'You don't need to tell me if you don't want.'

'I guess.' She shrugged and rubbed for a bit more and then thought, *Why not?*

'It's just… This is Grandma's farmlet, but it's mortgaged. Heavily mortgaged, for more than it's worth. There's no money. The bank's repossessing. They've given me another month, which considering the size of the debt is good of them, but after that, I need to be gone.'

'And you live in Melbourne.'

'I'm supposed to live in Melbourne, but if you can tell me what I should do with seven decrepit dogs, a dumb cow and calf, and chooks that are way past point of lay...'

'There are animal refuges.'

'There are,' she told him. 'And I've talked to them and they've told me frankly what chances my dogs, Grandma's dogs, have. The people running them are fantastic but they run on the smell of an oily rag and right now they're in trouble. The government's just made puppy farming illegal, with huge penalties. All the dodgy backyard operators are dumping their breeding stock before the new penalties come in, and there are so many dogs needing rehoming they can't cope. They've said they'll keep Grandma's dogs for a month and do their best to find them homes but they're not hopeful. None of my...none of Grandma's dogs are what you'd call cute. So after a month...'

She paused and rubbed Cordelia a bit more and struggled to continue. Forcing herself to think of the other animals. 'And a cow and calf like this? Scrawny, mixed breed, neither dairy nor beef? I might be able to find a place for the chooks, but the cows and the dogs...' She shook her head. 'Somewhere up there Grandma's breaking her heart and so am I.'

'Hey,' he said and her hand, which had been

rubbing with a fierceness that was almost desperate, was suddenly grasped and held. 'There are solutions. There must be.'

'You tell me what they are, then,' she said and tugged her hand away because a woman could only indulge in fantasy for so long and the time for fantasy was over. 'Are we done here? Let's go find your gear from the car, get cleaned up and get ourselves ready to face the day.' And then she shook her head. 'Or not. There's no need for you to face anything. I'll cut a hole in the fencing along the dry part of the boundary and you'll be right to go.'

'I won't be,' he said, almost apologetically.

'What?'

'The tree that came down last night,' he told her. 'It came down on my car.'

She stared at him in horror. 'On your car?'

'Right across the top. I haven't checked closely but from where I was standing when the tree came down…well, she won't be driveable.'

'But I thought…' Her heart almost seemed to stop as she thought of the implications. 'Your car… That tree… You could have been in it!'

'So I could,' he said, equitably. 'But I wasn't, which is why I'm doing the Pollyanna thing this morning. The sun's out, I'm not squashed, and there has to be a solution for all things.'

'I need to see,' she said, appalled, and he took her rags from her and gave Cordelia a farewell pat.

'Okay,' he warned. 'But it won't be pretty.'

It wasn't pretty.

So much had happened this morning that she hadn't even checked out the front of the house. She'd taken Bryn's word that the driveway was blocked and then been…distracted. They left the sheds, rounded the house and she stopped dead.

Dead. That pretty much described the massive gum that had crashed right across the driveway. In fact it had been dead for the last couple of years, killed by drought, or simply by old age. It had been the biggest tree on the property, a giant that even alive had been far too close to the house for comfort.

But there was no way Grandma would have cut down such a thing, and seeing it now, split, shattered, still smouldering at the stump, Charlie felt her eyes fill. She remembered it as a magic, living thing.

When she was eight years old her grandfather had fitted a rope ladder to the lowest branch. It had been a messy year. Her parents had been going through a vitriolic divorce and Charlie had been sent to Grandma and Pa's, 'to get her out of the way'.

Blessedly Grandma had decided that was exactly what Charlie needed. A place of her own. She'd been provided with armloads of comics, the kind her mother would never let her near. The first fork of the tree formed almost an armchair. Charlie had lugged cushions up there, hauled the rope ladder after her and pretended for a blessed while that the world didn't exist.

And now…

'A friend, was it?' Bryn asked and she looked at him in astonishment. What sort of guy guessed a tree could be a friend?

She shook her head, too emotional to speak, then gave her face an angry swipe. So much emotion. She needed to move on, letting the bank have what was left of this tree as well as what was left of this place. And the dogs and cows…

Did banks take dogs and cows?

And somewhere under this mess were the remains of Bryn's car. It had been squashed on her land while he'd been returning her dog who'd been wandering untended.

Could he sue? Of course he could.

How could you sue someone who'd been sucked dry?

Trying to fight off the wash of something dangerously close to hysterics, she edged towards the vast mound of splintered tree. The deluge of rain that had followed had stopped the whole thing being burned. There was still ancient foliage on the dead wood, the remains of vast branches with millions of leaves.

The car was on the other side of the trunk. She could just see. It was yellow. A branch had smashed down over the front but the body was still in…

In shape?

In the shape of a bright yellow, once stunning, Italian supercar.

Here.

She stepped back as if she, too, had been burned.

She'd seen this car, before her grandmother died. She'd driven from Melbourne for the weekend, and arrived as the guy had been leaving, a man in his sixties, smooth, urbane, wearing a suit that had screamed money. He'd given her a smile that had made her edgy—or maybe she'd already been edgy, what with a supercar parked in Grandma's yard.

'Good morning, Miss Foster. I'm Thomas Carlisle. You're earlier than we expected. Your grandmother told me you were coming today. Sadly I can't stay and talk, but do let me tell you what a wonderful woman your grandmother is. Clever, intuitive, forward thinking. It's been a pleasure doing business with her.'

And he'd gripped her hand, warmly, strongly, as if he'd had a right to hold her—and then he'd slid into his horrid yellow car and slimed out of her life. Out of her grandmother's life.

Leaving catastrophe.

'I've just invested a little money,' her grandmother had told her, defensive already. 'It's a solid investment and he's such an intelligent man. And he's a baron, Charlie—a proper baron. You're supposed to address him as Lord Carlisle, but he says "call me Thomas". He has a stately home and everything.

'He doesn't boast about it, though. I wish he could have stayed to talk to you but of course he's so busy. He has a brochure up in the general store and everyone's talking about it. Look.' She'd handed Charlie a glossy, gold-embossed pamphlet. 'See what I'm now part of.'

'Straws,' she said now, faintly, the sour taste of that conversation rushing back.

And Bryn, standing beside her, got it.

'You met my uncle, then?'

So she was right.

'Your uncle…' She whirled on him, fury threatening to choke her. 'That scumbag is your uncle? You're in that scheme that robbed half this neighbourhood of their savings, that made Grandma… that caused her…that…'

She could no longer get words out. She turned back and stared at the remains of one ridiculous supercar and all she felt was fury that the stump hadn't burned far enough to reach it. 'Get off my property,' she managed. 'I don't care that your car is wrecked. I don't care how you manage it. Get off this land now or I'll ring the police and have you carted away. Come to think of it I should ring them anyway. Your uncle…'

'Charlie, he's nothing to do with me.'

'No? Family business, isn't that what you said? *Your* family. So where is he now? He was supposed to have committed suicide, only the police say it was faked. They said he's probably in Brazil or somewhere, but wherever he is he'll be poncing round being Lord Whatever He Calls Himself This Week, selling these useless straws and talking old people into investing in his phony, cruel schemes.'

And then she paused. 'Or maybe he's still here. Is that why you're here? To help him get away? Whatever it is, I want nothing to do with it. Nothing to do with you. I don't care if you're covered in mud, Bryn Morgan or whoever you are. I've done with lying and cheating and I'm not as trusting as Grandma. I'm not even going to thank you for saving Cordelia. Or Flossie. Get off my land— or the bank's land—and get off now.'

And she turned and headed for the house at a run.

As Lord Carlisle of Ballystone Hall, Bryn led a privileged life. From the moment his grandfather had crumpled, had turned to him in shattered dependence, he'd decided the only thing he could do was to care for the vast estate, to pass it on—to whoever—with pride. He'd worked hard, hands on, doing what he loved. The lands had improved. The lot of the tenant farmers had improved, and the Ballystone stud cattle were starting to be known the world over.

Regardless, one thing Bryn didn't have to worry about was his creature comforts. There had always been a hot bath at the end of the day, excellent food, staff to see to details.

Staff was what he needed now. Help to get out of this mess.

He was filthy. His jacket was somewhere inside the house, blood-stained, abandoned after carrying Flossie in last night. He'd been wearing a light shirt, trousers and shoes, which had been enough while working hard with Cordelia but now... The sun wasn't strong enough to stop the cold. He was wet, muddy...no, make that filthy, and he was cold.

The farmhouse behind him looked firmly locked. He could still feel the echoes of the slam of the front door.

He raked his hair and a thick wedge of mud came away on his hand. Digging cows out of bogs was a filthy business.

He needed his phone. It had been in his jacket

pocket but he'd taken it out when he'd used the jacket to carry Flossie. It'd be lying on the passenger seat of the car.

He had a change of clothes in the car.

If he could reach the car he could get his clothes, get his phone, wash down in the shed and ring for assistance. He could even ring the police, and get the stolid local sergeant to explain to Charlie that he wasn't the scumbag she thought he was.

If she'd listen.

He wanted her to listen.

Why?

And strangely, tangentially, he was suddenly thinking…

No! The last thing he needed right now was emotional entanglement. Actually, the last thing he needed *ever* was emotional entanglement. The thought of loving someone else…

Just no.

But why was he thinking of that now? It didn't make sense, but he was.

When he was nineteen years old he'd lost his father, his uncle, his cousin and his twin sister, in the one appalling tragedy. The grief he'd felt that day was enough to last him a lifetime. During the ensuing years he'd tried dating—of course he had—but the moment he felt himself getting close that fear closed in. He held himself to himself.

But he hadn't held himself to himself last night or this morning. He'd held Charlie as if he cared.

He did care.

Why?

Because it was time out of frame, he told himself. These last few weeks, dragged into his uncle's sordid mess, away from home, away from anything that seemed solid, his normal defences weren't working. They'd be working soon enough. He knew that. But while they weren't…

'Pull back,' he told himself. 'Let yourself help, let yourself be a friend, but no more than that.'

'She doesn't want to be a friend. She thinks you're as bad as your uncle.' He was talking out loud.

'That makes it easier. She has no need of emotional connection and neither do you. What's happened last night and this morning was an aberration. Move on.'

So finally he shoved the thought of Charlie's anger away as best he could—and the emotions that went with it—and tackled what lay in front of him.

The tangle of smashed branches prevented any access to the car. A vast branch was blocking the passenger side. A smaller one lay across the driver's door, and one had slammed right across the engine.

He glanced back at the house. As he did, the curtains of the front window were hauled shut.

No help there. Not that he blamed her. What his uncle had done was horrific.

He'd thought Thomas only victimised farmers with Hereford herds. If he'd guessed her grandmother was a victim he would have explained earlier, but it was too late now.

But knowing what she was thinking…

Don't go there.

He needed to stop thinking of Charlie and focus. *Clothes. Phone. Car.*

He thought back to the shed, where Cordelia and Violet were presumably still recovering. While he'd been rubbing, he'd noticed an ancient scythe; like the ones tenant farmers had used to harvest crops a hundred years ago. He liked old tools.

He'd also noticed old saws. He didn't like them so much.

He looked again at the tree and he thought longingly of the well-maintained chainsaws in the vast outbuildings at Ballystone.

Beggars can't be choosers. When in Rome do as the Romans do. A bad workman always blames his tools.

Yeah, how many other platitudes could he think of? he wondered as he trudged back towards the shed. He'd obviously have plenty of time to think of them.

* * *

He was sawing his way into his car.

She shouldn't look. She was showered and warm and the doors were firmly locked and she should be over it, but she was still shaking with anger and she was still furiously aware that That Man was still on her property.

The bank's property.

She should call the police. They'd want to know he was here. She'd almost done her own citizen's arrest. He was stuck.

She was upstairs in Grandma's big front bedroom, edging the drapes aside just slightly so she could look.

He'd stripped off his shirt, or maybe it had ripped while he'd fought his way through the tangle of smashed wood. He was bare to the waist. He was sawing methodically, back and forth, long, even strokes.

The tools hadn't been used since Pa had died, almost ten years ago. She knew the saw would be rusty.

Excellent, she thought savagely. He'd have his work cut out for him. Even if it took him the whole day, that was a token recompense for all the pain his relation had inflicted on this community. On Grandma.

On her.

She headed back downstairs and fished in the

bureau for the glossy brochure Grandma had shown her. It was a magnificent production, with a picture of a stunning Hereford bull on the front, a beast even Charlie could recognise as something special. In the background was what looked like a little like a castle, ringed by mountains.

Once in a lifetime opportunity to gain ac-cess to sperm straws from the herd of Lord Carlisle of Ballystone Hall.

The brochure followed with a string of stun-ning comments from the UK's most respected farming magazines.

'What Lord Carlisle has done has pro-duced an advance in breed quality never be-fore seen in this country...'

There were links to articles astounded at what this breed was achieving.

And then the offer…

Straws of semen for sale under strict con-ditions. These straws are sold with condi-tions that each progeny will make a return to the company. If you don't wish to pur-chase semen, you have this once in a life-time chance to invest in this amazing breed.

Apparently Lord Carlisle had no desire to make more money himself but having set up his breeding herd at home he wished to see it expand into 'the colonies'.

There was sworn proof of testing, of stunning results from careful breeding. There were photographs of semen straws with the coat of arms of the Carlisles discreetly embossed on the outer wrapping. The straws had numbered certification of authenticity.

Included was a description of genetic markers to identify progeny and protect 'copyright', and enough science to make her eyes water.

There was enough promise of profit to make Grandma hand over what money she had and then head to the bank to borrow more. To a greedy bank manager in a small community who'd been dazzled himself.

It was all so stupid. So farcical. A decent Internet search could have exposed the scam before it began. But this was a depressed farming community, where drought and failing profits had eaten away its foundations. The young had mostly left, for the city and for secure jobs. What was left was a core of elderly farmers, struggling to make ends meet, struggling to keep their land. They'd been clinging to hope, and hope was vulnerable. This man had targeted them well.

By the time Charlie had realised what was

going on, the whole thing had been exposed. There'd been no need for Charlie to do any sleuthing—the police had done it for her. The real Lord Carlisle was said to keep himself to himself, an old man, almost a hermit, and in ill health.

The man calling himself Thomas Carlisle had obviously taken advantage, creating his own fraudulent online presence. Certification, paperwork, sperm containers, had all been stolen. Signatures had been forged. With no authority, he'd sold empty promises. Lies. Heartbreak.

The real Lord Carlisle had been contacted and was said to be appalled.

She headed to the Internet now and skimmed the recent media reports of the scam. Thomas Carlisle, real name Thomas Morgan… She hadn't even registered the name.

He was Bryn's uncle. Bryn was driving his uncle's car. He'd come to help a man who'd ruined lives.

Charlie sat at the kitchen table, her fingers seemingly paralysed on the keyboard. She was weeping.

These last months…the desperate call from Grandma… 'They're taking my land, love. The house… They're saying by the end of the week…'

She'd come down straight away, into a mess. She'd transferred what had been left of her own funds as a stop gap because she hadn't been able to see any other way of halting the bailiffs. She'd headed back to Melbourne to see lawyers…

And then the heart attack, the loss, the grief…

This man's uncle.

She'd kissed him.

Yeah, she'd been as naïve as Grandma.

She thought of him now, sawing with a rusty blade, trying to get into a car that must have cost far more than the value of this farm.

'I should ring every farmer in the neighbourhood and let them come to watch,' she said out loud, but she knew she wouldn't. Because the damage had been done, and maybe she understood now the way her grandmother had been conned.

'Because he smiles,' she muttered. 'And that smile… If his uncle was like him…'

She sniffed and sniffed again and then headed to the kitchen to cuddle Flossie, who was looking much perkier than last night. The bandage around her leg was still in place, looking almost professional. She thought of Bryn, of his tenderness as he'd cared.

'It's all a deceit,' she muttered as the rest of the dogs mustered in for a cuddle as well. 'How stupid am I? As stupid as Grandma, or stupider. He can saw out there for a month, I'm not going near.'

He'd been sawing for an hour when a truck pulled in from the road outside. There'd been a few cars pass, but the thought of flagging anyone down for help was daunting. But the rickety truck slowed as it passed, then did a U-turn and came into the yard.

An elderly farmer climbed out and stared at the mess in bemusement.

'What the…? You okay, mate? Charlie? She's okay?'

'She's in the house,' Bryn told him. 'She's fine. My car got squashed last night with all my gear in it.' He straightened and wiped away sweat. 'I don't suppose you have a chainsaw I could borrow?'

And then the guy saw the car and Bryn saw his face change.

How many people in this district had been conned?

'You're…'

'I'm nothing to do with him,' Bryn said wearily. 'I'm just returning the car to the…'

'He's his nephew! He came to help him!'

She must have been watching. Charlie's head appeared at the top-floor window. She yelled and the guy backed away as if Bryn smelled. Which, considering the mud and the sweat, wasn't surprising.

'What the…? You okay?' the farmer yelled up to Charlie. 'What's this low life doing here?'

'I'm fine,' Charlie yelled back. 'He's getting a taste of summary justice. Leave him to it.'

'He might be here for a few days,' the farmer yelled back and then he grinned. 'Couldn't happen to a better piece of... Yeah, I won't say it. Got a mess on my own place, love, but if you're sure you're okay...'

'Thanks,' Charlie yelled back. 'But I'm okay. Let's all mind our own business. This guy's nothing to do with us.'

She slammed the window shut, the truck did a fast reverse and Bryn was left alone again.

He sawed on.

In a way, the hard work helped. For the last week he'd been stuck in a dingy motel room or in the interrogation room at the police station, fielding questions from police, from accountants, from lawyers, trying to sort his way through a financial nightmare. His own lawyers had flown out in the end, and the mess was sorted as much as it could be, but the week had left its mark. He'd felt dirty even before he'd arrived here, and Charlie's contempt was making it worse.

What else could he do?

Years ago his family had abandoned the idea of compensating for Thomas's crimes. What Thomas had stolen, gambled, conned in his lifetime was enough to destroy everything they'd worked for and more. This scam had been a small one in the scheme of things, and it spoke of desperation. Thomas loved all things European. For him to spend months holed up in such an out of the way place, conning little people... He'd have hated it. And now he'd be in some even more distant country, conning more?

What could Bryn do about it?

Nothing, he conceded. The Ballystone Hall website, used only as a tool for marketing his cattle, was now plastered with warnings of this scam. It was hurting his own finances. People were now questioning the integrity of the Ballystone herd—with good reason. The last weeks had cost him a fortune. The idea of compensating every victim...

'You can't do it,' his lawyers had advised and they'd advised strongly. 'Your grandfather accepted it and you need to accept it, too. If you do it once you'll be admitting familial obligation, and you'll have every one of your uncle's victims from the last thirty years suing you.'

So he had to wear it, and it made him feel ill. Yesterday all he'd wanted was to get home and put this behind him. He couldn't bear to face the victims of Thomas's deceit.

He was facing Charlie.

Or not facing her. She was locked inside the house, hating him, hurting because of what his toe-rag uncle had done.

If Thomas were here now...

He wasn't. There wasn't a thing Bryn could do about his uncle. He had to put all his faith in international policing and hope that one day justice would catch up with him.

Meanwhile, could he help Charlie? Pay her out? He could do that without getting emotionally involved.

But the lawyers' warnings rang in his ears. 'One pay-out and you're liable for millions. Don't even think about it. Most countries have victims of crime compensation. We're sorry, my lord, but you'll just have to wear it.'

He was wearing it now.

All he could do was saw, and heave away dead timber, and feel…as if it wasn't even close to being near enough.

He was still on her land.

Three hours later he was still sawing, and Charlie needed to take the dogs for a walk, check the chooks and make sure Cordelia was doing okay. And get out of the house.

She couldn't sit in the kitchen and rage for the rest of the day. Or for the rest of the week. Or until the bailiffs came and repossessed Grandma's farm.

He'd sawed for a full morning. Maybe that was enough. What she most wanted was to get rid of him and the way he was going…her neighbour had said a few days. She wanted him gone now.

She looked out again at the mass of timber. He didn't seem to be making inroads. There was still a mess around the car.

Needs must, she thought, sighing. She had to let the guy off the hook.

How?

His phone must be in the car. Otherwise he'd have rung for help by now. If she lent him her phone he could ring for a tow truck, for a wood-cutter who was handy with a chainsaw—for a hire car? He'd have to pay—she had nothing to pay with—but that was his call. But she bleakly, finally accepted that she needed to approach him, maybe find the numbers, offer her phone, wait until he'd made the calls.

'Okay, Charlie, suck it up,' she told herself. 'Go lend the toe-rag your phone and give him the right numbers. Anything to get rid of him.'

But it took courage to walk out of the front door.

After her post cow-digging shower, instead of putting on another pair of ancient jeans she'd gone a bit formal. As a defence? Who knew? But for some reason it made her feel a smidge more in control. She'd pulled on black trousers and a crisp white shirt and she'd twisted her hair into a neat knot. Now that decision seemed sensible.

She was a career woman, and she knew how to handle conmen.

Or maybe not, but she surely knew not to do anything like kiss them. Idiots kissed conmen and she wasn't playing the idiot one moment longer.

Go and get rid of him. Fast.

CHAPTER FOUR

SHE LEFT THE dogs inside. If she let them out they'd be bouncing around her, joyful to be out and doing, and she didn't want their joy undermining her disdain. Bryn was at the far side of the bulk of the tree. She stalked around, fighting for courage. Keeping her disdainful face on.

And then she stopped.

He wasn't sawing into the car, or, if he was, he was doing it the long way.

What she hadn't realised from the glimpses she'd dared from upstairs was that he was working in from the far reaches of the driveway, unblocking the route to the house. He was forming a mountain of twigs and dead-leaf litter, stacking it well past the driveway. Anything that could be used as firewood he was stacking closer—where it could be loaded onto a trailer to be taken to a woodshed? He was clearing her drive as he worked.

Why?

He surely wasn't intending to drive his over-the-top sports car out. Even from here she could see it was damaged past repair.

Did he think she'd drive him?

That didn't make sense. He was giving himself hours of extra work, when surely the best option was to simply reach his car, reach his phone and call a cab.

She stared in stupefaction and, as if he sensed her presence, he looked up, saw her and stopped sawing.

'What are you doing?' she asked stupidly, and, even more stupidly, here came his smile again. In the face of all he and his appalling uncle had done, how he had the effrontery to smile…

To kiss her…

Do not think of that kiss.

'I'm sawing,' he said helpfully, and went back to sawing.

She stood and watched. He sawed as if the ancient, rusty saw he was using was brand new, built for the job. His strokes were long and steady, with no hesitation, no catching. Charlie had tried to use a saw before, and she knew it was hard with well-cared-for tools. To saw like this, with a rusty blade…

He'd said he was a farmer. Maybe it wasn't all lies.

But most of it was. She glanced again at the squashed car and thought of the damage, the pain. She hardened her heart.

'You don't need to clear the driveway,' she said,

and was proud of how cold she sounded. 'There's no way you'll be driving out. There's a local cab company in Carlsbrook. If you pay enough they'll take you to the airport. There's a guy who lives a couple of miles from here, a woodcutter. I've checked. He has more than enough work after last night to keep him busy for months but if you pay him enough he'll cut a path through to your car.'

He stopped sawing again and straightened, watching her.

'And where does that leave you?'

'That's not your business. I want you off my land.'

'Will he clear your driveway?'

'Eventually.' If she paid him. *With what?*

Don't go there.

'"Eventually" isn't good enough,' he said and went back to sawing.

'You can't clear it by hand,' she said, stunned, but he didn't pause as he answered.

'I'm thinking the bulk of it'll be done by this evening. By then I'll have reached my car. I'll retrieve my phone—and my gear with a change of clothes—and I'll do my own organising to get me out of here. And you'll be left with a clear driveway. So thank you for the offer, Miss Foster, but I don't need it.'

She was feeling…a bit dizzy. This man was a toe-rag. Why wasn't he acting like one?

Because charm was his middle name? She was beginning to realise just how her grandmother had been conned.

She was looking for the con now. She wasn't clever enough to find it but she knew it'd be there.

'I don't want you on my land any more,' she said, and it came out petty. Like a kid saying, 'I'm taking my bat and going home.'

He straightened again then, and set the saw aside. Once again she was caught by the sight of him. Naked to the waist, every inch of him toned, muscled, hard...

Was he really a farmer?

The way he handled that saw...

Do not let yourself be conned!

She walked forward, proffering the phone, holding it out as if she were handing over something distasteful to someone who was even more distasteful. As if she'd need disinfectant when she was done.

He smiled but his smile was rueful and he shook his head.

'I'm not taking more from you, Charlie.'

And what was there in that to make her blink? To make her eyes suddenly well so she had to fight back stupid, unwanted emotion.

Do not trust.

'Go inside and ring the police at Carlsbrook,' he said, just as gently. 'Ask to speak to Sergeant Marlow. I've been working with him for the last few days, trying to clear up what I can of this mess.'

'Of…your uncle's mess.'

'Yes.' He was looking straight at her, his gaze on hers, serious, steady.

Steady. It was a strong word but it resonated. In all this mess, he seemed somehow…solid.

Right. Grandma had thought that. Grandma had lost everything.

'Thomas Carlisle is an alias,' he told her, confirming what she'd just learned. 'He's really Thomas Morgan. My uncle. Once upon a time he was part of my family but that was a long time ago. He was wild as a youth, he was in trouble with the law before he turned twenty and he's gone from bad to worse. He broke my grandmother's heart. My grandfather died recently still despairing of him.'

'So you knew…'

'We've known for years that Thomas is a slime ball. We didn't know of this particular con until the police contacted us.'

His voice was deep. Even. Steady.

There was that word again.

'He's stolen from us,' Bryn said. 'From my family. From me. From everyone he touches.'

'He wasn't a Baron. A Lord.' She should have researched it herself, she thought wildly. She'd been so caught up in her personal distress.

'No.'

'And you… You really are a farmer?'

He held out his hands then, large, capable, worn. Hands that had carried Flossie in last night. Hands that had dug Cordelia out of the mud. Hands that had sawed for three hours without blistering.

'Farming's my life,' he said simply. 'I'm only here—'

'To rescue your uncle.' She said it flatly because it was the truth and she had to cling to it. Families didn't discard members. They stood together against the world.

Like she and Grandma. Going down together.

'I came because they told me Thomas was dead.'

That hauled her out of her introspection. It was a blank statement, bald, and it held her.

'Dead…'

'If you've indeed been conned by Thomas, you'll know he set this up with so much skill he might have got away with it.' His voice was suddenly tired. 'You might not know that he's conned people before. There are lawsuits against him at home and in half a dozen other countries. This was a small-time scam compared to the others, mostly I imagine because there are any number of law agencies looking for him. Now he's running out of options.'

Still he hadn't moved. They were thirty feet apart, a mile of distrust between them, and the bleakness in Bryn's voice seemed to make the distance greater.

'It seems, to give him time to get out of the country, he parked the car above the cliffs overlooking Deadman's Reach by the river north of Carlsbrook,' he said wearily. 'What a name, by the way—it's almost designed to live up to its reputation. He left a note saying he was tired of running, that he regretted his life of lies, that he was done. He left one shoe artistically at the cliff edge, and tossed another to land on a ledge below. He made scuff marks at the cliff edge and his briefcase wide open, so we could assume the wind had blown things away. He left the car, which he'd only leased. Leased with fraudulent papers. So I had a call…'

'You had a call?' She was struggling to take this in.

'I'm…' His voice faltered and something washed over his face—a shadow of pain? It was an impression only though, fleeting and gone before he continued. 'I'm pretty much his only relative. My father died some years ago and my grandfather recently. I couldn't ask my mother to come to Australia to prove her brother-in-law hadn't actually committed suicide but had taken off on yet another false passport to somewhere he could start conning people all over again.'

'You knew he wasn't dead?'

'I guessed. Once I was here I was sure.'

'That's what the police are saying,' she whispered. 'That it was fake. But you… You said you're here to help him.'

'I didn't say that. I've done as much as I can to undo the damage he's done but helping Thomas… If you knew how much I wanted to…' He paused and gazed around him, at her land, or the land that the bank now owned. 'No. Fury gets me nowhere.'

She shook her head, trying to rid herself of confusion. This man… Why should she trust him?

'The car…' she managed, looking at the wreck of the over-the-top sports car, and he sighed and even managed a wry smile.

'Yeah, that's my call.'

'Your call?'

'He used my name to lease it,' he said wearily, almost apologetically. 'That's another reason I had to come. I told you he's stolen from me. He came to my home…a while back and stole identity papers. Plus the rest. The car's the tip of the iceberg. It's…it *was* to be collected by the dealership in Melbourne.' He looked at it ruefully. 'It was hard enough to explain I wasn't responsible for the debt before it was squashed. Now…'

'You're responsible for that?' It was unbelievable. But suddenly…she did believe him.

Why? His uncle had been a consummate con artist. This man, with his blazing good looks, his smile… He was so far out of her realm…

Or he had been. But maybe Thomas *had* stolen from him, too, and she'd made him battle a fallen tree the whole morning and he'd saved Flossie and he'd saved Cordelia and…and…

She felt about two inches tall.

She could choose not to believe him. That'd be easier.

'If you need to keep thinking of me as a scumbag, go right ahead,' he said and, for heaven's sake, it was as if he'd read her mind.

'I don't get it,' she said, and she knew she was sounding desperate. 'How can I believe you're a farmer when you swan around in such a car? They cost…'

'I know exactly how much this one cost,' he said and named a figure that made her almost do a double take. And then, stupidly, the smile returned. 'But you know, life's not all mud. Sometimes a man needs to stop and smell the roses.'

'I don't know what you mean?'

'The police collected me at the airport and brought me here,' he told her. 'They put me up in the Carlsbrook Motel, which leaves a lot to be desired in the comfort department. I've spent days being grilled like a criminal. I had the distinct impression I'm lucky not to be behind bars myself and only the fact that I'd voluntarily flown out here gave them pause. Thomas has put my signature on a power of paperwork, and he's done it well. When they finally stopped suspecting me, I was still facing a mass of legalities. Finally I was cleared to go home but the police weren't offering to take me back to the airport. However, this car needed to be taken back to Melbourne. And what a car!' His smile became a grin then, suddenly pure mischief. 'So I thought…'

'You thought you'd just…'

'Have fun,' he said, but he said it quite gently. 'Because I've learned from hard experience that you can let grey overwhelm you, or you can catch at slivers of light.' He paused and watched her for a moment. 'I suspect there've been very few slivers of light in your life lately,' he said. 'Just how badly did Thomas hurt you?'

'You don't know details?'

'I don't know individual cons,' he said apologetically. 'The police seemed to think it was none of my business. They've cited privacy provisions, and, to be honest, I couldn't face knowing the details of every farmer he's hurt. He's done this before, Charlie. I can't undo—'

'Of course you can't,' she said hurriedly. What was he thinking, that she expected him to pay back every cent his toe-rag uncle had stolen? No one could do that.

'So tell me what's happened to you,' he said.

'You don't need to know,' she muttered and scuffed her foot on the gravel of the driveway, and Bryn set his saw down and walked around the fallen tree until he was in front of her. Right in front.

He put his hands on her shoulders and gripped, hard. She'd been staring down at her shoe, at the groove she was making in the gravel. She couldn't look up.

'Charlie...'

'Don't.'

'Please, will you tell me?' he said. 'I need to know.'

'Like the police said, it's not your business.'

'It just got personal. Charlie...'

'Okay, he took everything,' she said and the desperation was back in her voice. She couldn't stop it. 'He came in here because this looks like a farmhouse but of course it's only twenty acres because Grandma sold off the rest of the farm when Pa died. She did that so she could feed her waifs and strays. So she only had one cow and one calf and even Thomas had to concede she couldn't use one of his semen straws on such small, scrawny cows. But that didn't stop him explaining what a fantastic scheme it was. He told her what she was doing was marvellous and he wanted to help, so he'd offer her a once in a lifetime opportunity…'

'Hell.'

'It was hell,' she whispered. 'Because she still had an overdraft facility that's been sitting there from the time this was a working farm and the bank manager at Carlsbrook is lazy and has never checked. No one even queried when she withdrew a sum that I can't bear to…' She shook her head. 'No matter. It's done.'

'Oh, Charlie.'

'Yeah, and it seems Grandma wasn't the only local with stupid overdraft limits. Head office put the heat on the local bank manager and suddenly Grandma was in so much trouble. I managed to cover enough for her not to be evicted straight away but it was never going to be enough to keep her here. So she was appalled and grief stricken and then she had a heart attack.'

She shoved back then, away from his hold, anger and grief overwhelming her. 'And then she died,' she managed. 'So that's that. And I'm sorry. I'm sorry about your uncle and I'm sorry about Grandma and the dogs and the cows and my business but I'm darned if I can see a silver lining anywhere.'

'Then why don't we make one?'

She'd been close to tears. Very close. She could

feel her whole body trembling but Bryn's unexpected response brought her up short.

'What…?'

'It seems to me that we've both had a few tough weeks,' he said. 'So what should we do about it?'

'I…' She blinked. 'I have no…there's nothing…'

'Nothing silver lining-ish?'

'Lining-ish?'

'I'm from the old country,' he told her. 'I suspect we have a far more extensive vocabulary than you colonials.'

She didn't doubt it. That voice… It did things to her.

Do not go down that road.

'If you're relenting on making me walk off the property, I might grant myself a break from wood-chopping,' he was saying. 'But it's no use heading back into the house and sitting over a cup of tea playing who's the most miserable.' His voice softened. 'I concede, by the way. You are by a long shot. I've just been messed around by my uncle. You've lost your grandma.'

'You've missed your plane.'

'I have at that. But I've decided, right this minute, that it doesn't matter.'

'Of course it matters. I can call a cab. There'll be another flight tonight.' And then she paused in horror. 'But you didn't turn up. They'll charge you for another fare. Oh, my…'

'I've already thought of that,' he said, suddenly smug. 'Travel insurance. I'm a man prepared, and accidents are covered, which pretty much takes care of a car squashed by a lightning strike. So that's my flights covered. Though I'm doubting they'll cover the car.'

'What will you do?'

'Not panic,' he said firmly. 'Because panic does nothing. Instead I'll ring the collection agency and remind them that they did agree to me driving it back to Melbourne. Via email. They were relieved at the offer because it meant they didn't need to send their people to retrieve it. So my people can talk to their people while I focus on the important things in life. Like silver linings.'

'Your people?' she queried.

'Lawyers.' He hesitated. 'Where are your people?' he asked.

'I don't…'

'Your mum. Your dad. Your boyfriends, girl-friends, neighbours…'

'You saw one neighbour…'

'For two minutes and then he was off. Leaving you with a mess and someone he thought was low life. Just how alone are you, Charlie Foster?'

'I have the dogs.'

'Right.' He was surveying her thoughtfully. 'The dogs. And chooks and cows. They need to be included in our silver lining.'

'I don't know what you mean?'

'Meaning what, right now, would make you happy?'

'A home for the dogs?'

'You don't want to keep them?'

'How can I? I have a studio in Melbourne.' For which the rent was overdue already.

'Okay, too hard for today,' he said, still watching her face. 'What we need is something immediate.' He stood and gazed around, at the undulating hills, at the vast gums in the distance. It was a perfect rain-washed morning.

'It's a morning for doing,' he said.

'You've already been doing. You need to catch a cab.'

'I could,' he agreed. 'Leaving you with a squashed sports car, a driveway full of dead tree and other problems so assorted I can't begin to understand. But I've decided that walking away isn't the action of a hero and I've always wanted to be a hero.' Then, at the look on her face, he grinned. 'Come on, Charlie. You've been had by Thomas, but for every villain there has to be a hero. Ask any decent movie-maker. I know I should have donned a cape, called on my superpowers and cleared this tree in an instant, but you'll just have to settle for what you can get. And what you've got is my decision not to go home and leave you in this mess.'

'There's no need…'

'There is a need,' he said and he reached out, lifting her chin so her gaze was forced to meet his. 'It's Saturday and even superheroes need weekends. So how about we take the weekend as our silver lining and let the world break in again on Monday? What about it, Charlie Foster?'

'I don't…what are you suggesting?' She was reaching the point where she was too flummoxed to answer.

He gazed around again, and then focussed on the now massive heap of dead-leaf litter and mess he'd hauled away from the stump itself. The sun had been up for hours now and the rain-soaked mess had steamed itself dry. There was not a breath of wind. It was as if the storm last night had been a figment of their imagination.

'Bonfire,' he said in the tones of a small boy, suddenly fired with excitement. 'This lot would burn like firecrackers. We might need to phone your local fire brigade to warn them but…there's no rule against it, is there?'

'I…no…' At this time of the year half the locals were burning off to make undergrowth safe for the summer bushfire season.

'There you go, then. And we could have baked potatoes for lunch. Or maybe make that dinner. It might take a while to burn down to hot coals.'

'You want to stay for dinner?' She was having trouble making her voice work.

He'd been surveying the leaf litter but now he turned back to her, his eyes holding hers, warm, reassuring—and so, so compelling. She could see why Grandma had fallen for Thomas' charms.

She was wiser. Of course she was. Oh, but this smile…

'Let me stay,' he told her. 'Charlie, I want to help. I want to finish clearing this mess. I want to get the car off your land. I want to make sure Flossie's okay and that Cordelia's recovered from this morning's adventures. More, I want to see if there's any other way I can help.'

'Thomas was…only your uncle,' she managed. 'And he's hurt you, too. You don't need…'

'But I want to, Charlie,' he told her. 'So you have a man before you asking to be a superhero.' His grin widened at that. 'I'll admit I might be lacking in the Lycra department, but are you a woman intending to say no?'

That grin…that smile…

It was too much. The strains of the last few weeks were almost overwhelming but right now…

A superhero minus Lycra? She was close to laughter but also close to tears. Hysteria was edging back. But Bryn was weaving a spell with his smile. Offering her a silver lining?

Or just a bonfire.

It might be…fun.

Where had that word been lately? she thought. And where would it be in the future?

Take it now.

Bryn was watching, waiting for her decision.

'I don't have any potatoes,' she said, because right now the only imperative seemed to be the truth.

'That little blue car behind the house…is that yours?'

'I…yes.' She'd have to sell it, but she wouldn't go there now.

'Then let's do what you offered to do last night. Cut the fence in the top paddock and break out. Let's head into town and stock up on provisions and then come back and start our weekend. Potatoes on me,' he said grandly.

The thought of her car was put aside. This man was buying her potatoes? What an offer. She was forced to chuckle.

'Isn't your wallet in the car?'

'My wallet's in my back pocket, a little soggy but intact. There's the difference between me and superheroes in Lycra. How many of them have back pockets?'

She choked but struggled to stay with…sense. 'Your wallet has enough for potatoes?'

'Even for a bottle of wine.' His smile widened and it was as if the sun had come out. But the sun was already out, she thought wildly. She was delusional. She was becoming mesmerised by this man's gentleness, his smile, his…

Trustworthiness?

Don't go there. There was no reason at all for her to trust, she told herself. He was asking nothing except to be allowed to buy potatoes and wine and make a truly excellent bonfire.

Somehow she forced herself to pause, making herself examine the offer from all angles. She didn't trust. She couldn't.

But she did want time out. A bonfire. And wine.

And this man for a weekend?

Oh, for heaven's sake…

But the thought wouldn't go away and the grey had suddenly lifted from her world. It'd descend again soon enough, she thought, but for now…

'Okay, let's go chop holes in fences,' she said, a trifle breathlessly, and his smile gentled. Changed…

'Excellent. Very excellent decision, Charlie *bach*.'

And then, before she could begin to guess what he intended, he took her face in his hands. He tugged her forward and he kissed her.

It was a feather-kiss, no more, a mere brush of his mouth against hers. It had none of the passion of this morning. It was no promise, no hint at foreplay, no indication of anything to come. It was simply a kiss of tenderness, a contract sealed between two who might become friends. A mark of darkness past, with silver lining to come.

He pulled away and he was smiling again.

'Do you have anything in the house I could wear?' he asked, almost apologetically. 'I'm not exactly presentable. I could send you into town on your own but it doesn't seem a very superhero sort of thing to do.'

She *could* go on her own. It'd be sensible.

But suddenly Charlie wasn't being sensible. She was being the very opposite of sensible. That kiss...

She had nothing left to lose, she thought, and the kiss had fired a warmth in her that she hadn't felt for far too long.

Ever?

But enough of introspection. There seemed magic all around, and suddenly she was taking it. She had her very own superhero for the weekend and there was no way a woman would leave a superhero behind while she went grocery shopping.

She thought of him carting her groceries out to the car and suddenly she was almost blushing. Oh, for heaven's sake...

'There might be stuff of Grandpa's,' she said slowly. 'Grandma never threw things out.'

'Excellent,' he said and he took her hand.

'Okay, Charlie. Find me something to wear and let's have fun.'

And who could resist? Not Charlie.

The world was grey but for this weekend, the world was…hers?

What had he done?

He'd promised to stay for the weekend.

He'd kissed her again! Why?

His defences were right down, smashed by shock, betrayal and the bleakness of the last weeks. Somehow he'd have to build them again.

But he glanced at Charlie, at her face, at the beginning of a tremulous smile. He felt her hand in his.

Defences would have to wait until Monday.

CHAPTER FIVE

HE DIDN'T JUST buy potatoes. Once in the general store at Carlsbrook, Bryn suddenly became… someone who'd drive an Italian supercar?

Not exactly, Charlie thought, as she followed the trolley propelled by this man on a mission. He was wearing his own pants because nothing of Grandpa's had come close to fitting. They were liberally mud-spattered. One of Grandpa's sweaters had stretched beyond recognition over the years, and was now large enough to encompass his broad shoulders. It was faded and there were moth holes in the sleeves. His shoes were so filthy she couldn't see where mud ended and leather began.

He looked like a down-at-heel farmer, who hadn't bothered to change into his going-to-town best before leaving the farm.

But despite his clothes he didn't look like a down-at-heel farmer. Sure, he was wearing what looked like mucking-out-the-pigsty gear. Yes, he looked weathered, his eyes crinkled in the way of farmers the world over, men who spent too long in the sun and wind and rain. Yes, the hands hold-ing the trolley were farmer's hands, big, worn, capable…

But the way he held himself… He was tall, tanned and ripped, and despite his clothes he'd had the girls at the checkout a-twitter from the moment he'd walked in.

And as Charlie headed for the potatoes, he turned stubborn and headed for the delicatessen section.

'First things first,' he decreed. 'Entrée. What sort of cheeses does this place stock?'

Good ones. There were a couple of top-notch cheese producers in the valley and the supermar-ket stocked them for passing trade. Not for locals. No farmer around here could ever afford them.

But it seemed Bryn could. 'Excellent,' Bryn decreed and bought six large wedges.

'Six!' Charlie's eyebrows hit her hairline. 'We can't eat six.'

'You're talking to a man who's spent the morn-ing being a lumberjack. Watch me.'

She watched in stupefaction as he proceeded to load the trolley with enough food to feed a small army—an army with very specific and expensive dietary requirements. And part of her was joyful.

Ever since that first panicked call from her grandmother and the transfer of every cent she possessed, she'd been pretty much living on homemade soup and pasta. Now Bryn was loading up steak. Sausages. Lamb chops. Bacon. Butter. Nuts and crisps. A frozen apple pie. Cream. Beer. Wine. Even champagne. Oh, for heaven's sake…

'There must be caviar around here somewhere,' she muttered as he tossed in vacuum packs of smoked salmon.

'Really? Shall I ask?' Bryn turned to the girls at the checkout counter. 'Miss Foster's looking for caviar. Are we in the right aisle?'

She choked. The girls at the registers looked at her and looked at Bryn and decided the question was too hard to answer. Instead they giggled.

'Just how long are you intending to stay?' she asked faintly as a cabbage landed in the trolley on top of the champagne. A cabbage?

'As long as it takes,' he said enigmatically. 'Baked potatoes… We need tinfoil and sour cream and bacon and coleslaw but I have a feeling one cabbage is not the total coleslaw ingredient list. Suggestions?'

She stared at the pile in the trolley. 'You're planning to stay…how long?'

'Our bonfire won't be coals until tonight and I haven't eaten since breakfast. The steak's for our very late lunch.'

'The salmon…'

'Snacks,' he said enigmatically. 'Lumberjacks

get hungry. No caviar? That's a shame. Does your hardware section run to saws?' he asked the girls. 'Big ones?'

'Bryn, you can't…'

'I can.' He stopped then and turned to face her. They were in the middle of the vegetable aisle, surrounded by cabbages. A couple of middle-aged women were watching with unabashed curiosity, as were the girls on the register, but he didn't appear to notice. His attention was all on her.

'You're too alone,' he said, loudly enough for anyone—everyone—to hear. 'There's not a lot I can do to repair the damage Thomas has created but what I can repair I will. I don't have the money to compensate every victim of every scam but on a personal level… I wish to leave you enough wood to keep you warm for as long as you have here. I wish to clear your driveway. I wish to help you find homes for all your grandma's assorted dogs and cows and chooks. And most of all… Charlie, I want to make you smile. Thomas robbed you of your grandma and a whole lot more. I don't have to be back in the UK for a few more days. Let me do this.'

And then he held up his hands in a gesture of surrender, as if acknowledging there was more that could be read into what he was saying and he wished to back off.

'And, Charlie, it's potatoes and salmon and

coleslaw only—as long as I can discover how to make coleslaw. Nothing else. I'm not here to press unwanted advances…'

'What does that mean?' one of the checkout girls demanded of the other.

'Means he doesn't want to sleep with her,' the second girl said. 'Pity. If he asked me…'

'I can give you a great coleslaw recipe,' one of the shopping ladies volunteered, and smiled at Charlie. 'Charlotte, you go for it. You know your grandma would have wanted you to.'

'He's Thomas Carlisle's nephew,' Charlie said helplessly. 'He's admitted it. Thomas Carlisle. The guy who called himself Lord Carlisle. He stole from all of us. Why should I trust him?'

There was silence at that while Bryn was assessed. Clearly Grandpa's ancient sweater didn't fit with the remembered Thomas and his sleaze and his car and his lies. And then one of the checkout girls spoke up. 'I know about this guy.'

Everyone turned to her. Or maybe not Bryn, but Charlie wasn't looking at Bryn. She was trying very hard not to look at Bryn.

'I mean…' The girl seemed embarrassed with the attention and her friend had to elbow her in the ribs before she could continue. 'I mean…you know my dad's a cop? He said the creep's nephew has been here. They thought he was in the scheme too, but he came all the way from the UK to say he wasn't. This guy must be him. And he's gorgeous, miss,' she said in a hurry. And then she subsided as her previous pale complexion transformed to bright pink blush.

'You might be interested in the special on fancy coffee in aisle two, this week only,' her friend ventured, manfully trying to deflect attention from her friend's blushes. 'Just saying. If you're getting fancy stuff you'll need good coffee. And we do have saws. Any hardware you want. Anything else?'

'Dog food,' Bryn said, seemingly not the least perturbed. 'If you can point us to dog bones…'

'I'll show you,' one of the shoppers said warmly. 'And then I'll give you my coleslaw recipe. Oh, Charlotte, we were so worried about you.'

You still should be, Charlie thought wildly. I'm in such trouble.

The next few hours seemed to pass in a blur. They drove home and Bryn cooked them both steak for a late lunch. Steak—and he'd even bought enough for the dogs! Then Bryn headed back to the tree.

'Let's get ourselves a really big pile and light it at dusk,' he said. 'Do we need to notify your fire authorities that the mother and father of a burn is about to happen? Can you do that?'

Charlie did what she needed to do, then went out to help.

She had six dogs bouncing around her and she carried Flossie in her basket. Bryn had checked her leg and was happy enough to go without vet's advice. By now Charlie was trusting enough of his farming and animal experience to take his word.

'I'm thinking she might even be up to a bath tonight,' Bryn had told her as he'd reapplied the bandage. 'If we're gentle.'

We?

The word seemed to be seeping around her heart, on one level comforting, inviting, even seductive...

On another level, deeply scary.

Of all the things she didn't need in her life right now it was another man complicating things.

Except he wasn't complicating things. He'd saved her dog. He'd bought her enough food to last for a week and he was sawing his way to a clear driveway, free of charge. He was being a friend, so the least she could do was stop quibbling and go help.

As she walked down the driveway, loaded with dog, he didn't look up. He'd stripped off to the waist again. He was halfway through sawing a massive limb. His movements were rhythmic, even hypnotic—and that was how she felt. Hypnotised. By a beautiful body?

She couldn't afford to be hypnotised by anything—or anyone. But the day was gorgeous, the sun was on her face, the dogs were happy—even Flossie was wagging her tail. She had something to focus on other than the relentless worry and grieving that had been her life for the last few weeks. Or longer…

And she had someone to do it with. Someone like Bryn.

Don't think about Bryn. Do what he's doing: focus on the job at hand.

Yeah, right. A girl could work and look at the same time. A girl could work and feel.

A girl would be nuts not to.

He had company. Charlie.

Bryn was working with an excellent saw, and it made a difference. It should be making rhythm easy to maintain.

It wasn't. He was distracted.

Charlie had set Flossie's basket under a nearby tree, positioning it so she could poke her head into the sun if she wanted, or curl back into her basket into the shade.

She was a dog who'd run away. The gate was wide open now but she wasn't even looking at the gate. She was snoozing. Her fellow dogs were frolicking around her. They were occasionally stopping by to give her a conspiratorial sniff, but

Bryn was sure there were no break-out conspiracies happening.

Why would there be? He glanced again at Charlie and his saw faltered as if it'd caught a knot in the wood.

It hadn't. The falter had been his call entirely.

Charlie was collecting armloads of fallen branches, small stuff, carrying it out into the midst of the paddock, the place he'd decreed would make a great bonfire setting.

She was dressed in old jeans, a faded windcheater and wellingtons. Gum boots, he'd been told when he'd bought some from the general store. Charlie's grandpa's feet had been just a bit smaller than his so he'd splurged.

'You can't spend all of this,' Charlie had expostulated and he'd thought of how little gum boots cost and how little Charlie's debt would be in the scheme of things. He'd wanted to write a cheque right there. Only his lawyer's stern decree had stopped him.

'One payment and you admit liability. This is a no-fault situation unless you do anything stupid.'

They'd probably think chopping up dead trees on one of the victim's farms would classify as stupid.

It didn't feel stupid. It felt good.

Charlie's copper curls were tied back with scarlet ribbon into a…a what? A ponytail? It bounced as she walked.

She was whistling, a happy, tuneless little whistle. It was a good sound. No, it was a great sound. The dogs were bouncing around her and he thought, She's making them happy.

And then he thought of her last night, of her fear, and he knew things hadn't been happy for a long time.

Even before his scumbag uncle had made things worse?

Maybe he was imagining things, but he didn't think so. Something about Charlie mirrored Flossie's misery—something spoke of long-term weariness, almost defeat.

He shouldn't be staying on. He'd pretty much forced himself on her but there was something… something…

About the way her ponytail bounced?

It wasn't just that. Surely it wasn't. There were plenty of attractive women back home and he was sure lots of them had ponytails. One hint to his mother and he'd have a bevy of ponytails lined up for his inspection. She was desperate for him to move on but he wasn't interested. Since the tragedy on the estate, he'd steered clear of any serious relationship. Love hurt. Ponytails could keep their distance.

But this one…

It wasn't guilt that was keeping him here, he conceded. Even though this scam of Thomas's was a bit different in that it had directly involved him, he was pretty much over feeling guilt about his appalling uncle. 'That man was born evil,' his mother had told him. 'I have no idea why. He was born into such a lovely family but your father says he was born wanting to hurt people. He's given your grandparents such grief. Do what you need to protect the title and put him out of your mind.'

He did. He had.

So why was he still here? Why not just arrange someone to pay to do what he was doing?

Because a bouncy ponytail was whistling across the paddock towards him. She saw him looking and paused and smiled, and that smile…

It was enough to make a man almost break the saw on the next knot.

It might even be enough to break through the fear he had of relationships.

Um…not. But it was enough to make him think: There are things in this woman's past, and I need to find out what.

At dusk they lit their bonfire and it was pretty much the most spectacular bonfire Charlie had ever seen. The evening was warm and still. The mountain of dead leaves caught and blazed, sending sparks sky-high and radiating scorching heat.

Bryn had lit the base and stepped back. And stepped back again. And stepped back again and again and again.

Until he reached the spot where Charlie had set up a picnic rug—actually two picnic rugs because there were seven dogs who thought rugs beside bonfires were meant to share.

'It'll be an hour before we have enough embers to bake potatoes,' Charlie said, offering a bottle from a capacious basket. 'Want a beer?'

'And crisps and cheese and biscuits,' he agreed and flopped down beside her.

He'd pulled on her grandpa's sweater again. Some time during the afternoon he'd finally managed to access the car. He now had his own stuff, but he'd only brought business gear, plus a cashmere sweater for the plane—and this wasn't the night for cashmere sweaters.

He was filthy. It had been a day of hard physical work, and it felt…excellent.

He poured wine for her and a beer for himself and sat beside her and looked at the fire and felt…

As if this were home?

There was a crazy thought. Home was on the far side of the world. Home wasn't here.

This woman was here.

This woman who he'd met less than twenty-four hours before.

'Tell me about you,' he said, not for something

to say but because he suddenly very much wanted to know. Needed to know?

'I'm hungry,' she said and loaded a cracker with Camembert and popped it into her mouth. There followed a couple of silent minutes while the Camembert was given due reverence and then she smiled. 'Now I'm not quite so hungry. But I do need more. Is that Stilton? Wow!'

'There's possibly more to you than the fact that you're hungry and you like cheese,' he ventured and she smiled.

'I like sausages and baked potatoes, too. And wine.'

'A woman of depth. But—'

'Tell me about you first,' she said, hurriedly.

Yep, he thought, that's a woman thing. A learned thing. Ask a guy to talk about himself and the conversation's pretty much taken care of.

So what to tell her? How much?

He sat and loaded his own cracker and drank some beer and thought of home, of the vast estates, of the title, of the responsibilities that went with it.

But he didn't want it. Okay, the land, the cattle, the estate, they were things he loved, but the title should never have come to him. Baron Carlisle of Ballystone Hall... Lord Carlisle... His grandfather's death had made it all slam back. He'd had the title for a mere two months, but its inheritance had made the whole tragedy of the past slam back.

And now… Charlie had been scammed by a title. How to tell Charlie that was who he was? If she'd done a thorough search of his uncle's background she might have discovered that Morgan was the family name of Baron Carlisle, but she obviously hadn't searched that far.

Did she really want to know?

She was scoffing cheese, savouring every mouthful. She had dogs draped over her legs. The firelight was playing with her hair, making the copper curls glint. This was time out of frame for both of them.

To announce his title…he couldn't bear to. He could tell the truth without it—as he'd like to live the rest of his life without it.

'Okay, potted history,' he told her. 'I'm a farmer. My family's run beef cattle for generations. I love farming. It's in my blood—it's who I am. I'm thirty-five years old and still single, much to my mother's disgust but that's the way I like it.'

'You prefer your own company?'

And there was another decision.

He paused and thought about all the flip answers he could give. None seemed appropriate.

What was it about this setting, this time, this woman…? He rarely spoke of the tragedy that underpinned his life. He couldn't tell her about the title but the rest, with Charlie it seemed right.

'There was…an appalling accident when I was nineteen,' he told her, softly, almost tentatively. Exposing a wound that could never heal? 'I guess it's taught me that solitary is best.'

'Oh, Bryn,' she said softly. 'You want to tell me about it?'

Did he? Somehow it seemed he had to.

'I was away at university,' he said, talking into the stillness. Staring at nothing in particular. 'My sister was studying, too, but she'd come home for the weekend. Like many farming families, my grandfather, my uncle—my dad's older brother, not the one who scammed you—my dad, and my cousin Alan were sharing the farm, the land, the work. Our farm's large. Normally it's more than enough to support two families—plus my grandfather—but right then we were struggling. It was summer, there'd been a drought, and the huge underground water tank we used for house water had finally emptied. Just as it did, a massive storm came in from the north, with the authorities predicting a huge dump of rain. So my father and uncle decided to work in a hurry and clean it. They used a petrol-driven pressure pump.'

'Oh, Bryn, no…'

She got it, he thought. How many people would? But then, she had the advantage of knowing a tragedy had happened. His family had had no such warning.

Bryn had been interested in how things worked since birth. The rest of his family, not so much. It had become a standing joke. By the time he was ten years old it was standard practice… 'The tractor's stalled. Go get Bryn.'

But he'd been away at a house party with university friends. It had been Sunday morning, and there had been no one to tell them that their plan was dumb.

More than dumb.

Tragic.

'The fumes made them pass out,' he said, trying to keep bleakness from his voice. 'They would have died quickly as the fumes would have built and built.'

'Oh, Bryn…'

'There's more.' He closed his eyes, trying to block the scenario. The nightmare.

Say it like it was.

'Sunday lunch,' he managed. 'They didn't come home. My mother, my grandfather, my cousin and my sister…they were all waiting. So Alan and Louisa—my cousin and my sister—went looking. They saw my dad from the top—my uncle was further along the tank. We guess they assumed my uncle had already gone for help so they rushed down the ladder but by then the fumes had built up so much…' He shook his head. 'I guess…the only thing…the only thing that helps is that it would have been fast.'

He stopped. Was there no way he could ever shake off the grief, the guilt that he hadn't been there, the aching loss of so much of his family? Knowing he never could. 'I don't think you ever get over something like that,' he said at last and it was all he could say.

'Oh, Bryn, I'm so sorry.'

'It's okay,' he said brusquely, even though it wasn't. Even though it could never be okay. He shrugged. 'So there you have it. My uncle and my aunt divorced early so there's only Mum and me. We don't live in grief all the time but it's always with us.'

'She lives with you?'

'Um…not.' He smiled then, laughter unexpectedly resurfacing at the thought of his eccentric mother. After years of dreariness she'd found ways of distracting herself from a grief-ridden past.

'There's a scary word I'm sure exists for cases like mine,' he said, 'and it's called matricide. Mum is…well, matchmaking's probably too small a word for it. When she hits me at breakfast with a list of potential brides, she's in danger of being choked on her toast. And she likes…pink. She lives in the d— in a cottage next to the main house now, where she can pink to her heart's content and we get on much better. She doesn't hit me with brides until lunch time and by then I've had coffee and can handle it. I listen politely and then head back to the cows.'

There was a long silence. Charlie seemed to be taking it in, internalising. After so many reactions, so many years of hearing so many platitudes, so many appalled reactions, he found himself grateful.

'So your scamming uncle?' she asked after a while, quietly, and he was grateful. Past tragedy wasn't to be dwelt on.

'The uncle who died was my dad's elder brother,' he told her. 'The Thomas who scammed you was younger. Apparently he was a wild child, a wilder young man and eventually he turned criminal. We've seen him on and off over the years but only when he was after more money. He broke my grandparents' hearts. This last scam…' He shook his head. 'It's unforgivable. I'm so sorry.'

'It's not you,' she whispered and her hand slid silently into his.

And that felt…amazing. It was a simple gesture, a momentary act of empathy and why it made him feel…

He didn't understand how it made him feel. He disengaged because he didn't need sympathy, but loss of her hand felt like another grief.

'Enough of me,' he said, almost roughly. 'Fair's fair, Charlie Foster. Tell me about you.'

'There's little to tell.'

That was a deliberate deflection. She wasn't used to talking about herself, he thought.

'You said you're an interior designer.'

'You wouldn't think so, to look at me.' She looked ruefully down at her grubby, dog-hair-covered self. 'But I am. Tell me about your house. What's the décor of your farm? Modern? Shabby chic? Don't tell me, I'm guessing authentic provincial?'

He smiled, thinking of home, of so many generations of taste flung together in so many weird ways. But he wasn't letting her off the hook.

'You,' he said firmly. 'So you went to university?'

'I did,' she conceded. 'What did you study?'

Honestly, this was like blood from a stone. 'I started an engineering degree with a bit of commerce on the side. I decided if I was to be a farmer I was to be a canny one. So who sent you to university?'

'I guess… Grandma.'

'Your parents?'

'They're not on the scene. Mum's an anthropologist. Dad's a professor of anthropology, which is how they met. He's in the US now, on his third wife, with seven children that I know of. I don't hear from him. My mum's currently in Brazil, still bitter over what she sees as Dad's betrayal. She sends me a card at Christmas.'

'That's tough.'

'Not so tough,' she said. 'Dad's family had money, though I gather Dad's share's dried up now. I'm guessing one paternity suit too many. But when I was young there was enough money to send me to the best boarding schools. I spent the holidays here with Grandma and Pa. I loved art, so Grandma and I sat down and thought about careers where I could use art to make a living. Grandma was…sensible then.'

'Not sensible for the last few years?'

'Increasingly dippy since Pa died. This place has never been very profitable and she was lonely and bored so she sold most of the land to set up an animal shelter. That meant she had a nice cache your uncle could steal—and of course the bank manager hadn't updated her overdraft limits after she sold the farm, so on paper it looked like it was still there as security.'

She was still steering around herself, he thought, pushing away the personal. So ask it straight out. 'Charlie, am I right or was there trouble even before your grandmother got herself in so much debt?'

'I was worried about her. She was getting older, frail…'

'Charlie…' He reached out and touched her face, the faintest of touches. Interrupting her words. Hauling her back to the personal.

'There was trouble in your world before,' he said and she flinched.

'How did you…?'

'I don't know. But I can sense…shadows.'

'Money hassles can do that to you.'

'So there were money problems before?'

She chewed her bottom lip. He refilled her wine glass and watched as the firelight flickered over the trouble on her face.

She wasn't used to sharing, he thought.

Why did it seem so important that she did share?

Why was it so important that she trusted him?

He sat and waited. The dogs were settled, content to lie on their rug and enjoy the warmth from the fire, the proximity of humans. Tonight even Flossie seemed content.

The silence deepened. He wouldn't press, he decided. He knew, deep down, that Charlie wasn't accustomed to talking about herself.

Her childhood must have been solitary. He thought of his own. His mum and dad had always been there for him, and he and Louisa had been loved. They'd had the run of the lands. The tenant farmers' kids had been their friends—were still his friends. His grandfather, his uncle, his cousin, had always been there for him. Home was a haven.

He looked around at the land Charlie must have thought was her home. It now belonged to the bank. Her grandmother was dead. She must feel… untethered?

That was how he'd feel if he lost Ballystone, he thought, and it didn't matter that Charlie's loss was twenty acres and if Bryn lost Ballystone it'd be thousands of acres. He knew deep down it'd feel the same.

'I was married,' Charlie said across his thoughts.

That was a shock. The words were blunt, harsh, and he wasn't sure where to take them.

'Do you want to tell me about it?' he asked, thinking he needed to back off. But he didn't want to.

'Not much.'

He nodded, and scratched the ear of a black and white fox terrier who appeared to be missing an ear. Possum. By now Bryn had learned all their names. It seemed Possum was called Possum because he was obsessed with the species. Any faint rustle and he was onto it. His lack of ear was evidence that the brush-tail possums around here were bigger than he was, and far more vicious.

'He was like your uncle,' Charlie said and her voice was little more than a whisper.

Like Thomas. Uh oh. But he didn't respond. Shut up, he thought. She'll tell you if she wants.

'How was I to know?' she said, flatly now, staring at the fire and not at him. 'I met Graham as I was getting started as an interior designer. He was older than me and gorgeous. He had a name in the business, and he was loving, totally attentive—and he loved my work. It was so flattering but what I didn't realise—what I was too stupid to see—was that he was marrying a workhorse. That's what he needed and that's what he got. He brought me into the business and I worked my butt off.'

'Oh, Charlie…'

'I was dumb,' she whispered. 'Young, naïve, stupid. I met him as I finished my course and he was trying to set up a glitzy interior-design studio for the rich and famous. What I didn't see was that I was simply cheap labour. I guess…he must have loved me at some level, but the bottom line was that he didn't have to pay a wife. He loved being the frontman, the guy out there wooing the clients. The hard work of sifting through fabric swatches trying to find a match, endless phone calls to suppliers, trying to juggle finances…not at all. But he expanded the business and I was too young and too stupid to object. You should have seen our premises—you have no idea how swank. Of course all of it was on borrowed money but I was so busy trying to keep clients happy I didn't realise what a house of cards it was. Then it started to get nasty and suddenly he was gone, with a wealthy client, with homes here, in New York, in Hawaii. Leaving me with debts up to my ears.'

'Like my uncle,' he said softly. 'The moral compass of a newt.'

'Never trust people with Italian supercars?' she whispered. 'I'll add expensive watches to that list. Titles and mansions and promises and lies… I'd just managed to haul myself out of the mess he landed me in when Grandma landed me in another. And now…' She looked bleakly at the dogs. 'Now it's not just money. These guys… I can't bear to think about it.' She sighed and almost visibly braced. 'But that's enough of bleak. Is this fire died down enough to bury spuds?

'Can we scrape some coals out a bit so we can cook the sausages? I'm still hungry. Come on, Bryn Morgan. Let's get on with our silver lining.'

So they did.

For the rest of the night there was no talk of lies, of cheating, of debt. No talk of the past. They ate. They lay on their backs on the picnic rug and watched the stars appear. Bryn had thought the stars back home were bright but these were amazing. Or maybe it wasn't the stars that were amazing.

Charlie was pointing out the Southern Cross, the Big Dipper, Orion's Belt, the Pointers, and he listened to her soft voice. He watched her hand gently pat Flossie's head—Flossie had somehow edged onto their blanket and her big, soft head was nestled in the crook of Charlie's arm…

The night was still and warm. The fire had died to a mass of embers, every now and then spitting a spray of sparks into the night, sparks that looked as if they merged with the stars. There was still heat from the fire, but it was a gentle heat.

They'd buried their spuds and then dug them up and eaten them and Bryn couldn't remember when anything had tasted so good.

Was it just that the past few weeks had been so bleak, filled with lawyers, police, investigators, the knowledge that his name had been used to con small people, people like Charlie…?

But Charlie wasn't small. She was warm and curvaceous and kind, and her hand was stroking Flossie and…

And this time it was his hand reaching out and taking hers. So both their hands were resting loosely on the dog's soft fur.

Charlie's hand stilled.

She could pull away. There was no pressure.

He would put no pressure on this woman.

What was he thinking? Where were his thoughts taking him?

He knew exactly where his thoughts were taking him. Or where they already were, and they'd been there from the moment he'd walked into this farmhouse and seen her, scared, defiant, brave. How many women would open their doors to strangers on such a night? And she'd been so joyous when it was Flossie, a misbegotten mutt that only someone like Charlie could love.

Someone like Charlie.

How much debt was she in? How much trouble?

She had a good career, though. She could walk away, leave these animals to refuges, wipe her debts with bankruptcy, take a paid job.

It was unthinkable.

He could help. Surely?

And then out of nowhere, the thought, and even as the thought flashed through his mind it was in his mouth, spoken, out loud. A wish.

'Charlie…'

'Mmm…?' It was a sleepy murmur. The day of hard physical work, then good food, good wine, warmth and peace was doing its work. Was that why she was leaving her hand under his?

Or was the link as important, as strong, as meaningful, as it was to him?

That was a crazy thing to think. How could it be making sense—but suddenly it did, and the words were there. Spoken.

'Charlie, I want you to come home with me.'

CHAPTER SIX

THE NIGHT STILLED.

Neither of them spoke. There seemed to be no words.

Charlie's hand still lay under his but it had stiffened. No longer was it loose, warm, trusting. It was as if she was waiting for…what? The axe to fall?

This woman had been betrayed, he thought. By her absentee parents, by her husband, by his uncle. She didn't trust. And how could she trust? What he was proposing was crazy.

It was crazy for him, too. He didn't do relationships. So why did what he was feeling now seem so different? As if the rules he'd held rigidly to for so long no longer applied?

'What…what are you saying?' she whispered at last and finally she drew her hand away.

He wanted it back. The link seemed more than important while he tried to sort what he needed to say.

What he'd asked had been a spur of the moment thought, an idea only, but this woman didn't need speculation. She needed facts, something solid she could trust. Trust was something he could offer but who knew if it'd be accepted?

He had to give her space. The linking of their hands was a pressure she didn't need, and maybe it formed an emotion he needed to back away from.

Facts. Right.

He thought of what he could tell her—he should tell her—who he was, the extent of his fortune, the power he wielded back home. And he thought of her words… *'Titles and mansions and promises and lies…'* She didn't need that. More, she couldn't trust it. What he needed to offer was something solid, with no embellishments. Something to take away the shadows, not add more.

She was still fixedly watching the stars. Thinking who knew what? He had an image suddenly in his head of a fawn he'd once found, separated from its mother. Trapped in briars. Watching him approach without moving, but with every fearful sense tuned to what was coming.

He'd managed to free it so it could run back to where it belonged. He needed to do the same here, but he didn't want Charlie to run. Whatever he offered had to be non-threatening.

'Charlie, I told you I'm a farmer,' he said and waited until he got a slight nod. It wasn't a committal to anything other than she'd listen, but it was enough.

'My land's been in my family for generations,' he told her. 'It's good land—no, it's great land—and it's prosperous. I'm what some would call a warm man.'

'A warm man…'

'Wealthy, if you will.'

'You've had to pay to come here,' she said cautiously. 'And lawyers…'

'Believe it or not, it hasn't dented my income.'

She was still staring at the stars, her body rigid. She couldn't trust, he thought, and his heart twisted. This woman…she seemed so alone.

'I could pay your debts,' he told her and he watched the rigidity increase, the way her face closed and he knew there was more than one reason why he couldn't go down that road. But he repeated the sensible one. 'My lawyers tell me, however, that if I pay one lot of Thomas's debts then I set a precedent. It'd mean I could be accepting liability for them all and no one's wealthy enough to cover Thomas's scams. But what I can do…' His hand touched hers again. 'What I'm free to do is be a friend. I can offer you a holiday in the UK on my farm. I can afford your fares easily. You could come…for two weeks maybe? I'm not sure of your work commitments. You could come for however long you can manage. But here's the thing. I'm also in a position to take your menagerie with me.'

'My…menagerie…'

He was thinking fast. How to make this offer seem…not ridiculous.

'I'm not sure about the hens,' he confessed. 'Charlie, could you bear to leave the hens behind?'

'There's a place that'll take the hens,' she managed, bemused, humouring the lunatic? 'A friend of Grandma's. A place that houses ex-battery hens, a lady who's passionate about chook care. For a donation…'

He smiled at that, liking that he'd crossed the first hurdle and made her listen. 'I doubt a donation to poultry welfare would count as legal precedent for settling Thomas's debts.' He couldn't resist. He touched her nose. Lightly. Just to see if he could make her smile back.

She didn't. She was still rigid.

'It's crazy,' she whispered. 'Seven dogs. Two cows…'

'Charlie, my farm's big enough for two cows to spend the rest of their days grazing to their hearts' content. I can put them with the rest of my herd, taking them out only when the bull has access. They'll cost me nothing but a little extra feed in winter. I suspect there's quarantine, but Cordelia's coped with being stuck in mud. Quarantine with her baby beside her should be no big deal.'

'You're crazy. It'd cost—'

'Shut up about the cost,' he said firmly. 'I've said I can afford it. You need to trust me on that, Charlie.'

Trust? She didn't. How could he expect her to? She turned and looked at him and then turned back to star watching. 'You're being... it's nuts.'

'No, it's fun.' He touched her nose again, willing her to lighten. 'Fun for you and security for the dogs.'

'I don't get it.'

'I have two plans here,' he said, unbelievably firmly for a man whose plans were building as he spoke. 'Number one is a holiday—a real holiday—for one Charlie Foster. Number two is finding homes for seven needy dogs, good homes, personally inspected and approved by that same Charlie.'

'You really are nuts.'

'I might be,' he agreed and thought suddenly of his mother's reaction when seven dogs were unloaded from quarantine crates at Ballystone. The thought made him smile. His mother would have kittens—and then she'd put the almost frightening power of aristocracy and her love of animals to the fore.

'Charlie, you haven't met my mother, and you need to,' he told her. 'She's crazier than I am about animals. The one thing our nation is known for is dottiness about dogs. I'm thinking Mum could organise a heartrending piece in our local paper, outlying Thomas's infamy. That'll get the locals in. Thomas might be a villain but he's *our* villain and the locals follow his infamy with morbid curiosity. We could add a picture of each of your dogs, saying that Thomas has robbed them of their happy ever after. If we add a lump-in-your-throat description of their backgrounds to go with them I'm guessing we'll have queues wanting to adopt. And my plan is…you and my mum can have fun vetting each potential owner personally while you have a break. Fun, Charlie *bach*. How does that sound?'

'It won't… We can't…'

'We can,' he said, and enough of star watching. He took her hands and tugged, forcibly so Flossie slipped sideways and Charlie was lying on her side facing him, with Flossie sandwich-squeezed between them.

'It will work,' he said strongly. 'My mother will love doing this. I'll love doing this. I'm promising good homes, Charlie, I swear.' He hesitated, knowing this plan had to be solid. 'And if we don't find them good homes, our farm is big enough to house them all.'

'Seven…you'd go nuts.'

'What's a dog or seven on a place as big as

ours? The place is already impregnated with generations of dog hair.' He grinned. 'Who knows?
They might even become cow dogs.'

'In your dreams.'

'Maybe, but it'd be fun watching them try.'

'You're nuts,' she said, dazed. 'The whole concept's nuts. But even if it wasn't…the dogs… I
mean, that'd be great but… I don't need to come.
Bryn, the cost…'

'I can easily afford it. I promise that, too.
What's more, Charlie, you'll have a return ticket
in your hand before you leave. No tricks. I'm offering you a break from everything you've been
facing here. A holiday on a farm that's just as
beautiful as this one, but different in so many
ways. Have you ever been to the UK?'

'I…no.'

'There you go, then. I have plenty of room to
put you up. By the way, even though I'm sure my
adoption plan will work I'm thinking of keeping
Flossie myself. I don't see why my neighbours
should get all the joy. And trust… Charlie, my
mother's house is two minutes' walk from mine
and if you don't want to stay with me then she'll
love to have you. Or if you're really unsure, you
can stay at a B&B in the local village. No pressure. So go on, Charlie, just say yes.'

She stared at him, incredulous. 'This is…'

'Sensible. Fun, too. More silver lining.'

'But why are you doing it? You don't need to feel guilty for what your uncle did.'

'I don't. I'm doing this because I want to. Yes, I feel bad about the way Thomas treated you, and that you've been having such a bad time even before his scam, but I'm doing this because it sounds fun. Charlie, if you stay miserable then you've been robbed of far more than money and pride. Don't let the toe-rag win.'

He hesitated, then motioned to the pile of stacked wood on the far side of the driveway, all that was left now of the towering gum. 'When lightning hit that tree I was within a hair's breadth of being pancaked, but if I'd been pancaked I would have been pancaked in an Italian supercar. That's because at the end of this dreary week, when the sensible course would have been to drive back to Melbourne with my lawyers, I thought dammit! This car was leased in my name and how many chances would I ever have to drive such a beast?' He hesitated again and then forged on. 'I guess…that's what my sister's death taught me. That tomorrow mightn't come. So… How many chances will I ever have to take seven dogs and two cows and one Charlie back to my estate and find them all homes?'

'Estate…'

'Every man's home is a castle,' he said grandly.

'You're not finding me a home.'

'Don't mess with my fantasy.' He grinned. 'Or it might not be fantasy. I could ask Mum to put you in the newspaper, too. One fabulous interior designer, slightly dog-stained but very, very beautiful…'

'Don't…'

'Okay, we'll cut the beautiful. The picture will be worth a thousand words.'

'My home's here. I mean…in Melbourne.'

'Of course it is,' he said, gently now, his smile fading. 'I know that. But for the next few weeks… Seeing a bit of England. Finding the perfect home for seven dogs…'

'It's crazy to go all the way to England to find homes for seven dogs.'

'Crazy but fun. Wouldn't it be fun, Charlie?'

She was looking at him as if he were a sandwich short of a picnic. 'But to say you'll keep them all…'

'That's a fall-back position but it's still no big deal. My mother will love them and so will I.'

'She sounds…'

'Fun.' He was repeating the word but it seemed important. 'Despite her shadows, she's incorrigible. Charlie, come home with me and meet her.'

'But…'

'No buts. Just come.'

She stared at him in the moonlight, totally bemused. 'You're crazy,' she said at last.

'Granted.' His smile came back. 'But what's the alternative? Are you committed to work as soon as you leave this place?'

'I…no. I need…to find a new apartment. So much…'

'Right,' he said, moving on. 'What's a couple more weeks, then? And what's the alternative, Charlie *bach*?'

'What…? Charlie *bach*? You called me that before. What does it mean?'

'Charlie dear.'

'You're kidding. Don't call me that.'

'Why not?'

'Because it makes me feel…it makes me feel like I don't want to feel.'

She was looking straight at him, her eyes wide in the moonlight. There was a long silence. Things were changing. Massive things.

He didn't do relationships. He didn't.

This though…the way she made him feel…

'Does it make you feel like you'd like to be kissed?' he asked, and it felt as if the world had stopped and was waiting for her answer.

She closed her eyes and he watched as she took a deep breath and then another. The world held its breath.

Something changed in her face. Twisted. Cracked.

Something in the whole night changed.

And finally she answered. One word.

'Yes.'

Yes. One word to change the world? For this night, it was the only word he needed.

He took her face between his hands and drew her gently, slowly, infinitely tenderly towards him.

He smiled down into her face, drawing out the moment, because something inside him told him this was important. This seemed precious, fragile, something that mustn't be rushed.

'Charlie, you realise this can't be like our kiss in the bog after rescuing Cordelia?' he said softly. 'That was an adrenalin rush, great but unplanned and you didn't know me. This time, you need to trust. So… Are you sure, Charlotte Foster?'

He'd had to ask. This was her home, he was an uninvited guest and she was alone and he wouldn't, he couldn't press. But trust… It was a huge ask.

But her answer was ready.

'I'm sure,' she whispered and she opened her eyes and smiled. 'You kiss me or I kiss you,' she whispered. 'Either way, Bryn Morgan, let's do it.'

He'd kissed women before. Of course he had. His mother had had potential brides lined up from the moment he'd hit his teens. Maybe even earlier.

But he was thirty-five years old and he'd never felt a kiss like this.

It felt right.

It felt as if his heart was being given right then and there.

The warmth, the heat, the wanting…

She moulded to him, with Flossie squashed somewhere between. It wasn't Flossie's heartbeat he was feeling, though. It was all Charlie's, and it felt as if their heartbeats merged in that moment.

Becoming one?

It didn't make sense. Nothing made sense, but right now who was trying for sense? Every nerve ending was focussed on one kiss. There was no yesterday, no tomorrow, no thought of anything beyond this moment, because right now, right at this moment, his world was changing.

Bryn Morgan, Lord Carlisle, Baron of Ballystone Hall, had always considered Ballystone was his home.

It wasn't.

His home was suddenly…here.

What was she doing? She didn't trust. She couldn't.

Okay, she didn't, but for now her world was on hold. She could stop trusting again in the morning. For now all that mattered was that Bryn was holding her. The fears, the distress, the weariness had disappeared. She wanted nothing but this man.

The kiss filled something deep inside, an aching void she scarcely knew she had. To draw away was impossible. It'd be like drawing away from life itself.

She felt herself melt into him and her body reacted with joy.

It was dangerous. She'd been down this road.

No, she hadn't, her body told her. She'd never felt like this. And what danger was there in melting? She was a grown woman. She'd take this one night…

So when he put her away from him, just a little, when he smiled down at her, his eyes dark with passion, with tenderness, with desire, when he said, 'Charlie, if we're to stop, we need to stop now. I want you more…'

'You can't want me more than I want you,' she said simply and put her hands on his face and drew him back to her. He'd take her to his bed, she thought, or her bed, although seven dogs might mess with even the most passionate lovemaking. And then a thought. 'Bryn, we don't have…'

'I believe I do,' he said, and his voice was different, husky, as if he wasn't so sure of himself. But the smile was still there, and the tenderness and…the need. 'I've sawed the car free and also freed my toiletries. Charlie, I'm thirty-five years old and single. My bag's ever hopeful.' He touched her lips. 'But this isn't hopeful. This is… different. Charlie, are you sure?'

And there was only one answer. This wasn't a dream because she already knew it would happen, and her body was reacting with joy.

Trust didn't matter, she decided, at least it didn't matter for now. Trust was for tomorrow. Tonight was for a man and a woman and nothing else.

'Yes, Bryn, I'm sure,' she whispered, and tonight started right now.

She woke in the small hours, when dawn was drifting in through the open window. She lay in Bryn's arms and she felt…loved.

It was illusory, she thought. It had to be illusory because she was a big girl now and she knew how the world worked. Trust was what you did before the world fell apart.

But her world had already fallen apart, so what the heck? She could lie here cradled in this man's arms, skin against skin, feeling loved, protected, desired.

She could let herself pretend.

And when he stirred and woke and smiled sleepily at her, with passion already kindling behind that gorgeous smile, when he said: 'So what do you think, Charlie love? Will you trust me enough to come home with me? With your dogs and your cows and…you?'

When he smiled at her in such a way, she thought how could trusting hurt her any further? A couple of weeks with Bryn in England? Letting him in some way compensate for his uncle's scam? He didn't need to. The plan seemed crazy, but if he could afford it, what did she have to lose?

She could lose her heart, a small voice whispered, but she blocked it out. Which was really hard to do when he was smiling at her in such a way…

It's just for two weeks, she told herself, striving desperately for sensible. She'd be simply giving herself time out and in the process giving Grandma's animals their only chance of good homes.

And what was her alternative? She was facing eviction from her studio. She needed to find a job, pick up the pieces of her life, but two weeks wouldn't make a difference.

And if a part of her…a really big part…was saying two weeks' time out, time away from here, time exploring his farm, time seeing the real Bryn…

Well, that was a dangerous thing to think. That scared her, but at her heart she knew she wasn't sensible at all. A sliver of light had entered her bleak world.

The sliver was hope.

But he was waiting for an answer. Waiting to smile at her again. Waiting to take her back into his arms and show her...how joy felt.

So what was a woman to say?

Will you trust me enough to come home with me?

'Yes,' she whispered as she sank back into his arms. 'Yes, I believe I will.'

He was taking Charlie home for two weeks.

Two weeks only.

There was a part of him, a huge part, that was hoping it'd be for more.

But one step at a time, he told himself over the next few days. She didn't trust and why should she? There was the whole thing about his title. He should tell her now, but he knew instinctively that it'd be asking too much to put that on her. Not now. Once she found out... Well, the airfare was flexible. If she hated what he was—as he still hated it—she could always return, or use her ticket to see a little more of England. She'd see her animals safe. They could both move on.

What was it about her that made him feel bleak at the thought?

He thought of his mother. She'd reacted with almost ludicrous excitement when he'd told her he was bringing Charlie for two weeks.

'It's only for a holiday, Mum. Thomas has

cheated her and we can help. She needs to see her animals resettled.'

'But you like her?'

'Of course…'

And that was enough for Alice, carried away in extravagant hope.

Hope *was* extravagant, he thought. How could two weeks change something so deeply embedded into him, the fact that he walked alone?

But a part of him was questioning already, before his mother even asked the question.

Had his wall of loneliness already been breached?

There were formalities to be sorted before Charlie, seven dogs and two cows could travel. The bank was due to take possession of the farm in about three and a half weeks. She could leave then. Bryn, though, had to leave earlier. There were legalities from Thomas's scam that needed to be cleared and he needed to be home to do it.

But he did manage to spend four more days with her, and those days seemed to change him. Those days had him thinking the nightmare of his past might be something he could finally put away. It was too soon to say—of course it was—but each day he spent with her his life seemed lighter.

They worked side by side, sorting the detritus

of her grandma's belongings, clearing the remainder of the mess of the tree, cooking, laughing, loving. And as the days wore on, the more taking her back to the UK seemed the most important thing he'd ever worked for.

And yet, he couldn't tell her how important it was. He knew her trust was fragile. This woman had been betrayed. Even as they made love he could see the questions. When would this end?

When he told her he was the Lord Carlisle of the glossy brochures? When he finally revealed the title he loathed? He wasn't courageous enough—or stupid enough—to reveal that yet. He could only hope that when she reached Ballystone, she'd see for herself that Thomas's lie was his reality. That underneath the title and the wealth, he was simply a farmer she could trust.

For now he had to focus on practicalities.

Practicalities revealed problems. It seemed dogs could only be imported as pets, with a limit of four dogs per person. After a call to his lawyers it seemed easier to declare they were his dogs and his mother's, that he and his mother had bought them from Charlie and wished to import them to their new home. Charlie would simply be escorting them. That declaration involved more trust, and it seemed a major step when Charlie agreed.

There was another hitch. He was faced with a form declaring he and his mother had no intention of selling or disposing of the dogs. After reflection, there seemed no problem. He had many tenant farmers, and it'd take little organising to find them good homes on the estate. As a last resort, the dog pack at the Hall would simply expand.

He couldn't talk to Charlie about that, either. Telling her about his tenant farmers meant she'd have to know about his title. The prospect kept drumming through his head. How would she react?

As if it didn't matter, he told himself, but it was a plea inside his head. Please let her not care about titles. Yes, it'd be a shock when she reached Ballystone, but surely once there she'd see the estate for what it was, big, a bit ramshackle, a bit overwhelming but underneath…home? And even if she reacted with disgust, she'd have her return ticket. She'd have her holiday and her animals would be safe.

He had to shut up and hope. He wasn't risking her pulling back now, because every morning he knew he wanted her more. Leaving her, hoping she'd follow, was almost more than he could bear.

And it seemed she felt the same. 'I can't bear you to go,' she whispered on that last morning. 'This seems like a fantasy. I'll wake to reality.'

'You'll wake in England, with seven dogs, two cows and me. If that's reality…is that so bad?'

'Something will happen. You won't be there.

You'll turn to dust?' She managed a slightly shame-faced smile. 'I know. You're real and you've been wonderful and, Bryn, despite everything that's happened, this has been one of the best weeks of my life. But happiness doesn't last.'

'Yes, it does,' he said resolutely. 'It must.'

'When your family died…'

'Mum and I both thought our world had ended,' he told her. 'And so it had. It was the end of that world. But here I am, lying with a woman called Charlie in my arms and I'm thinking…a whole new world is ours for the taking. You want to join me in this brave new world, my Charlie?'

'It's only for two weeks,' she whispered, still fearful. 'It's…just a holiday.'

'So it is.'

'But I still can't believe it's real. Bryn… Just hold me for a while before you go. Let me have a few more moments believing this will happen.'

He held her and hoped she believed.

He wasn't sure that either of them did.

CHAPTER SEVEN

HE LEFT, AND what followed was three long weeks of waiting. They video-called and he worried as he saw her face, etched with the strain of packing, doubt that she was doing the right thing. Finally, though, she was in the air and he was driving to London to collect her.

The dogs were arriving on a later plane. The logistics of transporting seven dogs had been a nightmare. His mother was officially importing three dogs and Bryn was importing four. 'Tell me why I'm adopting three dogs?' his mother had asked faintly, and she'd watched in bemusement as he'd made a hash of trying to explain. She was confused? He felt the same.

But it *was* happening. The dogs would arrive three days later. That'd give Charlie time to find her feet.

Or get cold feet and turn and run before they even left Australia?

The finalising of dog flights had been Charlie's doing. He wondered if there really had been no room on her flight, or if the delay had been deliberate. Was she giving herself time to check him out first—was he who he said he was? Was his offer real?

She couldn't completely trust, he thought, not where her grandmother's animals were concerned.

For her to trust…

Maybe he should have told her…

But it was too late now. He was in the arrival hall, watching as each passenger emerged from the customs hall. The place was packed with excited relatives and friends. There were balloons, flowers, emotion…

He hadn't brought flowers or balloons, but emotion was there in plenty. That she'd trust to come all this way…

And then she was there, standing uncertainly in the doorway, in her standard uniform of jeans but in a new, fresh windcheater. She was dragging a battered roller suitcase behind her. Her curls were tousled and her eyes were shadowed.

She looked battered herself, he thought. Thinner. The last weeks had been tough and once again he felt the tug of remorse that he hadn't been able to stay and help her pack.

He watched her for a moment more, soaking up the sight of her, her presence, the almost primeval surge of joy that said his woman was here. His woman? Surely it was too soon, but that was how it felt as he edged his way through the sea of balloons and flowers and hugging relatives. Finally she saw him and her face broke into a smile he thought he'd remember all his life. Relief was there in spades, but there was more. There was deep, abiding trust and it worked both ways. As he reached her and gathered her into his arms he truly felt that he'd come home.

The moments from alighting from the plane, going through Immigration, waiting for the baggage carousel to do its interminable thing, had been some of the longest of Charlie's life. During the flight itself she'd felt almost numb. The last weeks had been filled with legalities, practicalities, emotion. She'd packed up the farm, putting the things she most treasured into storage. She'd done the same with her studio in Melbourne. She couldn't afford to keep it.

Everything she possessed was now in a tiny storage shed or in the suitcase she carried—or in quarantine in Melbourne waiting to catch a following plane.

How much trust did she have in this man waiting for her? When she'd boarded the jet in Melbourne she was so tired she could hardly think. She'd dozed her way to London, but when she'd landed, when the seat-belt light went off and her feet were walking, taking her closer to where

Bryn had promised to be, the sense of panic was almost overwhelming.

What was she doing, trusting this man to do what he'd said he'd do? Was she mad? She should turn around, get back on the plane and go home now.

But he'd offered her animals a home. She'd seen the paperwork. Their transport had been paid in full. And for her…this was just a holiday, she told herself. It was simply a part of his generosity. A two-week break on his farm.

But deep down, she knew it was so much more. She knew he wanted her.

Why?

What was the catch?

Stop it, she told herself as panic started again. He's just a farmer, solid, a guy who has enough money to make a wonderful, generous gesture. He's a guy who couldn't resist driving his sleazy uncle's supercar but, still, he's a guy with no frills. A guy with a smile to die for.

A man whose body made her melt.

But as she was waved through Customs, her feet seemed to be moving all by themselves. She was in some crazy dream. She'd been sucked in by that smile, that tenderness, that care, and who knew what lay in front of her?

'He's a farmer,' she whispered to herself. 'A farmer like Grandpa. He has a toe-rag uncle who's conned him like he conned everyone else but otherwise he's solid. Sensible. Kind.'

The doors slid open to reveal the sea of waiting faces, the balloons, the crowds waiting for their loved ones.

And then, across the sea of heads, she saw…a smile. A smile that said it was okay, no, more than okay. A smile that said that solid, sensible and kind didn't begin to describe this man.

A smile that said Bryn was here, waiting to welcome her home.

Home? That was a crazy thing to think, because this was only a holiday. In two weeks she'd go back to Australia, find herself a job, another place to live and get on with her life.

But Bryn was coming towards her, cutting through the crowd with ease. He was wearing what she guessed many farmers wore when they came to town—decent chinos, an open-necked, gingham shirt and a casual oilskin jacket. His smile creased his weather-worn face and lit his eyes.

He was walking toward her, a big man with quiet authority. He was smiling and thanking as people moved aside to let him through, but he had eyes only for her. The people moving might think his smile was for them but she knew…

And maybe the crowd knew too, because eyes were turning to her, to see where this man was moving. Were they sensing romance? Sensing a happy ending?

It was no such thing, she thought breathlessly, but then he reached her and his arms caught her and swung her high. He smiled up into her face, his eyes loving, laughing, joyous.

And then he tugged her back down and into him. His mouth met hers and the crowd around them burst into spontaneous applause.

But Charlie didn't hear. All that mattered was that Bryn was holding her. She was in his arms and, dumb or not, the sensation was totally consuming.

Charlie Foster had come home.

What followed was a gorgeous, peaceful drive back to the farm.

They were in his battered farm vehicle. 'Sorry, love, Mum has a meeting with the church ladies in the next town. She says she's very happy you're here, Charlotte Foster, and she sends a big welcome, but you're not seventy and you don't have arthritis so that means you get this and she gets the padded leather sedan.'

It made her chuckle. It made Bryn's mother seem…less scary. 'I need to warn you, she'll be matchmaking like mad. You'll have to wear it, I'm afraid. Like I've had to wear it all my life.'

She chuckled again. Bryn's mum didn't seem

a threat. The morning was gorgeous and she was sitting by Bryn's side taking in a world she'd never seen.

His farm was almost on the Welsh border, he'd told her, three hours' drive away. That was fine by her. By Australian standards it was close and the vehicle felt good. It smelled strongly of dog and other things, indescribable farming stuff. There was a box of businesslike tools in the back and the duco was liberally mud spattered.

'I should have got it cleaned for you,' Bryn told her but she shook her head.

'I like it the way it is. It smells…like Grandpa's truck. It smells normal.'

'And you the interior decorator.' He smiled across at her. 'I'm shocked. I hoped you might make a few suggestions while you're here about sprucing things up. For instance, this. Interior suggestions?'

'You mean…the car?' she asked cautiously and he grinned.

'I do mean the car. Let's start small. If you do a good job here I might let you into my shed by the end of your stay.'

'You'd let me decorate your shed? Isn't that sacrosanct?'

'Yes, but it's messy.' There were, in fact, many sheds, but he'd had one heated for use when he was mending things. Or pondering mending things. Guy's stuff, he thought and he grinned.

'You don't really want me in your shed,' she said and it was an accusation.

'Not until you've proved your mettle. Okay, the car…suggestions.'

She gazed around her at the battered vehicle that looked as if it had been used for years doing tough farm stuff. She couldn't think of a single thing she wanted to improve.

Like its owner. There was not a thing she wanted to improve there, either.

But he was waiting, smiling, daring her to suggest.

'Okay,' she said, bending her mind to the challenge. 'The first thing we need…you carry livestock in this car, right?'

'Right,' he said cautiously. Dogs all the time. The occasional calf.

'Okay, then pests are going to be a problem. I suggest a fly sticker.'

'A fly sticker?'

'A cute little yellow sticker that hangs from your visor and catches any bug that dares enter. Then I'm thinking dream catchers to match. Very tasteful.' She gazed around at the dog-hair-covered interior—he'd obviously made an effort to brush her seat clean but nothing was going to get rid of the evidence of years of dog occupancy.

'Then there's the dog hair,' she said happily. 'If you can't beat it, join it. I'm recommending faux-fur seat covers. I can order online if you like, maybe rainbow to match the dream catchers? Or faux leopard skin? That's practical. The dog hair will disappear so you'll never notice. You'll need two sets so you can toss one set in the wash if things get really messy.'

'You're…very kind,' he said faintly.

'Don't mention it. And then outside…' She stared thoughtfully into the distance, formulating plans. 'I know. We could transform it into an *oonce* car. How cool would that be? Driving over the farm ooncing like anything.'

'Um… Ooncing?'

'I've only seen a couple, in Melbourne on the nightclub strip late at night, but they're amazing. You need a powerful sound system, by which I mean head-blowing-off powerful, and rainbow-coloured strobe lights underneath that can be synced with the music.' Then, at the look on his face, she chuckled and relented. 'You think that's over the top? You may be right. Let's make it uni-coloured. Purple seat covers? Purple dream catchers? We can find strobe lights that make the entire underside of the car flash purple. The cows will love it. Imagine coming home late at night, across the fields, with your *oonce* car…'

'Why is it called *oonce*?' he asked faintly.

'Because that's what it feels like—*oonce, oonce, oonce*—like a heartbeat. It stays with you for weeks.'

'I can…no, I can't imagine…'

'And then your shed,' she said happily. 'Ooh, Bryn, I can't wait to get my hands on it. I think I'm going to enjoy myself.'

'Great.'

'You do trust me?' she said and twisted so she was looking directly at him. 'After all, I've trusted you to come all the way to England. The least you can do is let me convert a wee car.'

'If you really want to.'

There was a moment's silence at that. 'Really?'

'Really.'

'You'd let me?'

'Charlie, I trust you.' He searched for the biggest commitment a man could make. 'Even with my shed. Such is my trust.'

Wow, Charlie thought, and she sank back onto her seat and gazed ahead in stupefaction.

Trust…

This man…

Where was this going? She had no idea.

It scared her but there was something building inside, a warmth, a strength, a surety.

It wasn't to be trusted, she told herself, but there was that word again.

Trust.

And then they slowed and Bryn took a right-hand turn from the highway. The roadside sign said Ballystone Hall. And then, before she could respond, he turned again, through grand stone pillars and onto a private road.

Ballystone Hall.

The name was like a slam to the side of her head.

The brochure.

This was the seat of the Barons Carlisle and it was also the home of the magnificent Ballystone Hereford Stud. It was the place Thomas had used for his scam. Photographs of this Hall, this property, even the cattle she could see grazing in the distance, had been plastered over the glossy literature used to cheat and to swindle.

The Hall loomed ahead, a vast pile of grey-white stone, three storeys high, surrounded by sprawling lawns. There were acres of paddocks… no, fields…stretching away to mountains in the west. It looked as if it had been here for centuries, settled, magnificent, grand.

A stately home.

Ballystone Hall.

'Where…why are we here?' she stammered.

'Because we're home.'

To say she was stunned was an understatement. There were no words for how she was feeling.

She'd been looking forward to a comfortable

farmhouse, solid, yes, substantial even, as he'd told her money wasn't a problem. But this…

'Stop,' she whispered, struggling to get the word out.

Bryn nodded as if he'd expected this response. He came to a halt in the middle of the driveway.

Driveway?

Massive oaks formed a grand avenue, sweeping up to the Hall in the distance. It'd take ten minutes to walk the length of the driveway alone.

'Is this…?' She could barely get the words out. 'Is this where you live?'

'It is,' he said gently and then before she could get the next question out, before she could even begin to form the sentence, he answered it for her.

'I'm Bryn Morgan,' he told her. 'Charlie, I know I should have told you earlier but to be honest… I thought if you knew you might not come. So I am Bryn Morgan but I'm also a baron. Since my grandfather's death I'm Lord Carlisle of Ballystone Hall.'

The words were doing her head in. Thomas… Fraud… Ballystone Hall…

'Thomas…your uncle…he said he was Lord Carlisle.'

'Thomas was Thomas Morgan. He was my grandfather's third son. My father was second in line, so when he and his elder brother and my cousin were killed I became the heir. Morgans have held the Carlisle title for generations.'

'But… Lord Carlisle's in his nineties,' she managed. 'It says so on the internet.'

'I suspect the site you saw hadn't been updated, or you looked before he died. My grandfather only died three months ago. His death was probably hastened by the shock he felt at Thomas's scam. He was the Eleventh Baron Carlisle. I'm the Twelfth.'

'I-I have no idea of what's going on,' she stammered, staring out at the intimidating driveway. 'Bryn, you're scaring me.'

'The last thing I want to do is scare you.' He was watching her as a cat watched a mouse, she thought, even as she acknowledged her thoughts were verging on the hysterical. But that was what it felt like, that he was watching for what her next move might be.

There were lies everywhere. When would she ever learn?

'I haven't lied to you,' he said and that scared her even more. Could he read her mind? 'I thought…if I threw the title at you back in Australia…well, it still seems unreal to me and I wasn't sure how I could make it real for you. But I'm a farmer called Bryn Morgan, Charlie. Nothing's changed.'

'You're kidding.' She waved wildly in the direction of the Hall. 'How do I know anything's real? You've probably just rented this for the weekend. Or this is some sort of blow-up stately home you've hired from a theme park?'

'Why would I do that?'

'I have no idea, but nothing's making sense.' Her thoughts were swinging wildly but suddenly they focussed. 'The dogs,' she gasped. 'They're already kennelled in the transit holds. They'll be here in three days. I have to stop them coming.'

'Why would you want to stop them coming?'

'Because they can't come here.' She was staring at the Hall as if it were some sort of monster. That was what it felt like, she thought. It was as if the building itself were mocking her.

The last few weeks she'd felt the burgeoning of faith in this man, the slivers of light that said here was something, someone solid... But who was he? An hereditary baron. Lord Carlisle of Ballystone Hall. It sounded like a hero in a romance novel. He should be wearing breeches and cravat and riding boots, with valet in attendance.

She took a deep breath and made a valiant effort to be rational.

'So you own this place,' she said and was proud of the way her voice sounded.

'I do.' He was sounding cautious, as if not sure where to jump. That made two of them.

'And you're saying... You're Lord Carlisle.'

'I am.'

'But you call yourself Bryn Morgan.'

'I am Bryn Morgan.'

'Thomas called himself Carlisle—Thomas Carlisle.'

'Thomas is Thomas Morgan. He *is* my uncle. He used the name Carlisle to evade police, and also to make the use of the title seem more plausible.'

His answers seemed to be wafting over her head, an irrelevance. She was staring at the great house and remembering the glossy brochure with photographs of exactly what was before her now. Pictures of a historic mansion at the end of an avenue that was truly breathtaking.

The promise of money, money and more money.

'This *must* be part of his scam,' she whispered. 'The Ballystone Stud Herefords. Known the world over. What did he tell Grandma? A lifetime opportunity. Step right in, suckers, and let me bleed you dry.'

'Charlie…'

But she didn't want to hear. She'd been stupid to come. Stupid as she'd been stupid before. 'Just take me to the nearest railway station,' she said wearily. 'Or let me out here and I'll hitch but I'm going home.'

'What, now?' He had the audacity to sound bemused.

'Of course now.' The words were practically a shout and they reverberated through the vehicle with such intensity it shocked her.

There was a moment of silence while both of them seemed to take stock. But Charlie wasn't taking stock. She was concentrating on breathing.

Paper bags were good for panic attacks, she thought. Where was a paper bag when she needed one?

'I think,' Bryn said at last into the silence, 'that maybe you're overreacting.'

Overreacting? She looked again at the opulence of the place in front of her and thought underreacting was a better description. 'This place was used to con Grandma out of her life savings,' she muttered. 'And me. Can you blame me for not wanting anything to do with it?'

'Yes, this place was used,' he agreed. 'As my grandfather's title was used.' For the first time she heard a trace of uncertainty in his voice. 'Charlie, if I'd told you we were coming here, would you have come?'

And there was only one answer to that. 'No.'

'And that's partly why I couldn't tell you,' he said softly. 'Because it seemed desperately important that you come.'

He reached for her hand but she pulled away, as if the touch might burn.

For weeks now, ever since she'd learned the true

extent of Grandma's tragedy, she'd felt trapped. The sensation now was more of the same. A lot more.

She was stuck in his car. She was forced to listen.

'Charlie, I needed you to come,' Bryn was saying. 'Back in Australia this place would have seemed a dream to you, or, more likely, a nightmare. I knew you'd see it as part of the fraud. But I need you to see it as it really is. It's just…home.'

'You have to be kidding. How can this be home?'

'Believe it or not, it is,' he told her and his smile returned. It was a gentle smile, though. She was reminded suddenly of the way he'd treated Flossie that first night. An injured creature… Was that how he saw her?

'I only use one wing of this place,' he told her. 'I moved in to keep Grandpa company. Mum lives in the dower house.'

'The dower house!'

'Believe it or not, we have one,' he said. 'That's what I'm asking you to believe.'

'You've lived here for ever?'

'Yes.'

'But the scam…'

'Can I tell you about it?'

She glared. She crossed her arms across her breast and concentrated on glaring. 'Yes,' she snapped and a rueful smile lit his eyes. But then he started talking and the smile died.

'My uncle Thomas was, well, wild is maybe too kind a word for it,' he told her. 'Even when he was small he hated the farm. His life's been a constant of gambling, cheating, lying, living far above his means. My grandfather's always been more than generous but he's squandered everything he's been given. We haven't seen him for years. But last year he came to visit. He'd heard Grandpa was failing and wanted to see him. We let him stay because how could we not? But he badgered Grandpa for more money. There'd be money in Grandpa's will but he wanted it then. It seems he was in trouble with money-lenders— which might be the reason he ended up in Australia. But by then Grandpa was confused, too ill to respond, and I ended up hauling him bodily out of the bedroom. He spent the night abusing me, he got drunk on Grandpa's best whisky and then he passed out.

'The next morning he still seemed asleep so I left him to go check on the cattle. When I came back he was gone. It wasn't until the police contacted us that we realised he'd rifled the office, stealing empty semen packs, literature, the things we'd ordered in bulk when the herd started being recognised. He'd been careful to only steal enough so we wouldn't notice.'

'But…' She was still having trouble getting her voice to work. 'It doesn't…it doesn't matter. You told me lies.' She was holding desperately to her indignation. It seemed the only thing she had to cling to.

'I told no lies,' he said strongly. 'Not one. I'm a farmer, Charlie, first and foremost. I have boots and wellies and battered rain hats in the mud room. I have sheds full of farm gear, calving equipment, everything I need to make this place work.'

'But you're a baron.'

'You think I like that?' Unexpected anger blazed, his eyes darkening to almost black. 'You think I want it? My uncle was always supposed to inherit, and my cousin after him. Next in line was my father. And they all died and I was left. Even then there was my grandfather, the real Lord Carlisle. He's the only person I can think of when I think of the title. He was a kindly, gentle man, bereft from his losses, and while his death was expected it's still left me gutted. So, yes, Charlie, I'm a baron, but it took four deaths of people I loved for me to become one. So if you think that's an occasion for joy, for shouting to the rooftops that I'm the new Lord Carlisle—'

He broke off, seemingly drained, but still searching for words. 'And then there was my uncle Thomas,' he said wearily. 'He took my family's legacy and he smirched it. So the title…who wants it? Not me. You ask why I didn't tell you? Yes, I thought it might stop you coming but, at a deeper level, it's not who I am. If that's who you thought me, I'd be pulling you here on false pretences.'

She thought about that, or she tried to think. The muddle in her head couldn't be untangled.

His grief…

Don't go there. She had enough of her own to handle.

'So first you say if you told me I might not have come, and now you say I might have come *because* you're a baron?' she managed. He might be angry but she was angry too. And confused. He had his reasons, but he had deceived…

And she was in so much trouble. His smile, his explanation, the way he made her heart seem to twist.

But she couldn't be sucked in. Not again. This was so foreign to her, so crazy, so…unreal.

It *was* unreal, she thought, staring again along the avenue towards the Hall. Sure, this man told a good story and it might even be true, but to trust him… If she let herself be driven down this avenue, if the great doors opened and closed behind her…

The feeling of being trapped was almost overwhelming.

She wasn't being reasonable—she knew she

wasn't—but the betrayals of the past were all around her. Her parents. The smooth-talking liar who'd been her husband. Thomas…

'Bryn, I need to go home.' Somehow she steadied, and for a moment she felt a flash of pride that she'd managed to set the hysteria aside. 'I'm sorry.' She took a deep breath and turned to him, facing him square on. 'You…you've been wonderful. Crazily wonderful. You've done such a lot for me and you're offering to do more. What you've just said… I'm sorry but I can't be part of it.' She took a deep breath and struggled to explain further, for he deserved an explanation. She had to believe him enough to try.

'Bryn, my husband walked out on me two years ago,' she told him. 'Our marriage was never good but at least I trusted him. I was a fool. Then Grandma…she was good at trusting as well. Even my mum… She trusted my dad and his betrayal drove her out of the country. She's hardly been back.'

'You're still saying I'm like that?' The anger was still in his voice and she flinched. But she had to keep trying. She had to make him see.

'No, Bryn, I'm not.' She was trying to get it right in her own mind. 'But I don't know you. This…' She waved towards the Hall, and out over the land to the distant hills. 'This has been a shock but I think I needed that shock. Because I was about to jump again.'

'Into trusting.'

'Into loving,' she whispered. 'And that's the scariest of all.'

There was a long pause. A very long pause.

'You think you might love me?' he asked at last. It wasn't spoken like a lover. Anger still resonated.

'I can't.'

'Can't doesn't mean you don't.'

'Can't means I have to pull back. Bryn, it's too soon, too crazy, too unreal. I've been out of control for too long and sitting here staring at your gorgeous house, thinking of your life, even your trauma, I'm thinking here I go again, jumping into trust… Bryn, please, I need to go home. The animals aren't due to fly out until tomorrow. I can cancel their flights. Please don't stop me. I need to do it.'

'What will you do with the dogs?' Anger had been replaced with weariness.

'I have no idea,' she said honestly. 'But the worst-case scenario is the refuges and at least there they'll be treated with kindness until…'

'Until they're put down. You'd do that to them?'

'How do I know what'll happen to them here?' she demanded, confusion almost overwhelming.

'For all I know they'll be used here as... I don't know...fox bait?'

'As if such a thing was possible. Even if it was... Do you really think I'd let that happen?' Anger blazed, full force.

She was being unreasonable, unfair. She knew she was, but she was past explaining.

'No.' She fought for control again, for reason. 'Of course...of course I don't. But I can't...'

'Trust.'

'That's right,' she said wearily. 'I'm sorry. But please take me to the nearest transport back to the airport. I'll repay you for the flights. When I can.'

'There's no need.'

'There is a need.' She closed her eyes, aware of a wash of fatigue so great it terrified her. Was she being stupid? Maybe she was, but there was nothing she could do about it. 'Bryn, please.'

'There's nothing I can say?'

'Nothing.'

There was silence for a long time. She felt his frustration. More, she felt his anger. Because she couldn't trust?

It couldn't matter, she thought. She had to find her feet again. Somehow.

And Bryn knew it. He swore, very softly, and then he turned on the engine.

'Okay, Charlie,' he said bleakly. 'Let's get you back to the airport.'

And then he paused. A car was pulling up behind them. A big white sedan, glistening in the morning sun.

It had turned into the avenue a bit too fast and skidded to a halt as the driver realised the way was blocked. The driver's door flew open and a woman emerged, little, buxom, dressed in an electric-blue frock, a startling pink jacket and heels that were far too high. Her silver white curls, piled into a messy knot, were embellished with streaks of the same electric blue as her frock and she came running towards the car with a beam a mile wide.

'Oh, help,' Bryn said.

'Help?'

'If you thought you were trapped before,' Bryn muttered, 'heaven help you now, but you're about to meet my mother.'

'Charlie!'

Normally when Bryn met his mother after an absence his reaction was to flinch. And then brace.

His mother was, to say the least, full-on.

Those meeting her for the first time might have said Alice Morgan was eccentric and maybe she was. Her eccentricity, however, was a shield. He knew it. The loss of her husband and her daughter had almost destroyed her but somehow she carried on. She faced the day with a beam a mile high, and her warmth and generosity were legion. So instead of bracing right now, Bryn climbed out of the vehicle to deflect her from diving right in to hug Charlie. And as he did he found himself hoping…

When all else fails, bring in the big guns.

His mother.

'Is she here?' She tugged back from him and peered into the car's interior. And saw Charlie. 'Charlotte…' Her beam turned full on as she headed for the passenger side of the vehicle.

Charlie emerged to meet her, looking stunned. What had he done to her?

Alice was enveloping as much as she could into an embrace. Charlie wasn't big but his mother was tiny. Bryn came from a family of big men, and they'd been the ones to pass on their genes. His mother's genes of little, blonde and bubbly were all hers.

'Dear girl… He wouldn't let me ring you,' Alice was saying. 'I wanted to, to tell you how welcome you were, but Bryn said it'd be pressure on you to come and it wasn't fair. A two-week holiday? How wonderful. And he did pass my message on about the dogs? That they're so welcome? And so are you. You did know that, didn't you?'

'I…yes, I did.' Charlie was still being hugged but Alice had pulled back a little and looked at her critically.

'Oh, my dear, you look exhausted. Those awful aeroplanes. I went on one once. Ugh.'

'You flew to Edinburgh for Great Aunt Edith's eightieth,' Bryn said mildly. 'You were in the air for an hour.'

'Totally discombobulating,' Alice agreed. 'I had jet lag for weeks. What you need is a nice bath and some tea and then a sleep. Bryn hoped you might be staying at the Hall but honestly, dear, it's a cavern. You could fit a family into every bedroom. The dower house is much cosier. I think the peony room. I've just had new curtains hung—isn't that lucky?'

'Mum, Charlie's not staying,' Bryn said and that brought silence.

Alice paused and her eyes did a thorough search. On the surface Alice Morgan might appear to be bubble and fluff but underneath there was piercing intelligence. She was looking at Charlie now and Bryn knew she'd be seeing the exhaustion, but beyond that… The shock. The fear.

'Oh, my dear, what's happening?' She wheeled about to face Bryn. Accusing. 'She's scared. Charlotte's scared. Why?'

He held up his hands in defence. His mother was all accusation. 'I just… I might not have told her how big the Hall was.'

'Or that he was a baron,' Charlie whispered.

She gestured helplessly at the amazing avenue and the miles of lush farmland stretching to the mountains beyond. 'Or any of this. I thought... I thought he was a farmer.'

'And so he is a farmer,' Alice said roundly. 'A foolish one, though. Bryn... Are you mad? The first time I saw it I almost had a palsy stroke. Come and meet my family, your father told me, and we ended up here. For high tea. With a butler, even! Thank heaven we don't do that any more but this place is still enough to scare a girl out of her senses.' She turned back to Charlie. 'You have to grant that my son's heart's in the right place, though. It always has been. When he rang and said we were adopting seven dogs—'

'But you're not adopting,' Charlie said helplessly. 'He said...you were organising homes...'

'I guess we are,' Alice told her. 'Homes here. Did he show you the paper we had to sign that said we had no intention of getting rid of them? That's the immigration rules. We need to bring them in as personal pets. I had to sign too, because there's restrictions on numbers. Not that I mind. The dogs here have a very good time and...' she waved an inclusive hand '...we appear to have enough room. But enough. Why is Bryn saying you're going home?'

'Because I don't trust him,' she said wildly. 'All

of this…' And she wheeled on him. 'The dogs… advertising…you said…'

'It was what I thought,' Bryn said apologetically. 'It was only when I downloaded the formal papers I realised. But it doesn't matter, Charlie. We have many tenant farmers who may wish to take on a dog with such a story and if they don't, then, as Mum says, we have plenty of room.'

'You didn't tell me.'

'And he should have.' Alice put her hands on her hips and glared. 'Why didn't you?'

'I wanted Charlie to come,' he said simply. 'Charlie, I couldn't risk you not coming.'

'It was so important?' his mother demanded.

There was a pause. He met Charlie's look full on. She was looking bewildered, angry…so many emotions. He wanted to gather her and hold her but the time for that wasn't now.

The anger he'd been feeling had faded. There was only Charlie and there was time only for a simple truth.

'It was so important,' he said gently. 'It was the most important thing I've ever wanted in my life. That you come.'

She was so confused.

Where did she take it from here?

In a romance novel this should have been the happy ending. If she took one step forward she knew she'd be enfolded in his arms, cherished, held…

Held.

There was the rub. Held?

How could she risk being held?

Her heart said it wasn't a risk at all, but her heart had betrayed her before, as her mother's heart had betrayed her, as had Grandma's heart. Trust was such a fragile thing and the consequences of it failing were enormous.

He'd lied to get her here. Or…okay, he hadn't lied but he might as well have. He'd deceived by omission. Leaving out the bits that'd scare her.

She was so bewildered, so tired, so…

'Let her be, Bryn.' Alice edged between Charlie and Bryn, doing her best to block out Charlie's view of Bryn—hard given that Bryn was over six feet tall and Alice was barely five. In heels. But she was insisting that Charlie's focus had to be on her. 'You need to leave everything aside,' she said. 'Everything that Thomas has done to you and everything that my son has said or not said, or done or not done. Bottom line? Bryn tells me that seven dogs are booked to arrive here in three days' time and two cows a little time after. Yes or no? Bryn?'

'Yes,' Bryn told her.

Alice nodded. 'There you go. I've seen the documentation. Charlie, do you believe that's happening?'

'I...yes.' She was having trouble getting her voice to work.

'That's a start,' Alice said. 'So right now you don't need to trust any further. Here's the suggestion. Forget my son for a while.'

'Forget...

'He has plenty to do without bothering you,' Alice told her. 'For the next few days, come and stay with me, in the dower house. Bryn can leave you alone. He can spend a bit of time reflecting on his folly and think about what he's going to do about it, but that's up to him. What I suggest you do now is rest. A long, hot bath, Charlotte, and don't tell me you don't want one. I can see it from here. Aeroplanes are horrible and Bryn says you'll have been exhausted before you left. Then you can spend a few days pottering around the estate, doing a lot more resting. In three days we'll receive the dogs. Bryn will collect them from the airport and get the paperwork sorted.'

'I will,' Bryn said helpfully from behind his mother.

Charlie thought, Is that laughter back in his voice? She cast him a suspicious glance but he was back to being bland again. And...concerned.

The concern seemed such a part of him. An intrinsic part of who he was.

Dared she trust it?

'Just do it,' he said now, gently. 'Charlie, let my mother take over for a while. You don't need to trust. You just need to take your bath and potter and let events unfold.'

'I can stay in a B&B,' she said, feeling foolish.

'You can,' Bryn said and that smile was definitely back in his eyes. 'That's a step better than going all the way back to Australia. But Mum has a guest bathroom to die for and she's aching for a guest. Isn't that right, Mum?'

'Why would you stay in a B&B when you can stay with me?' Alice demanded and tucked her arm through Charlie's. 'Go away, Bryn, and herd some cows or dig a post hole or something to vent a little spleen.'

'I don't need to vent some spleen.'

'Yes, you do, dear,' she told him. 'I can tell. Go away and let me talk Charlie into taking advantage of my truly sumptuous bathroom.'

She gave in. Of course she did. Demanding to return to Australia on the next plane was an overreaction. She'd stay until the dogs arrived.

She lay in the Baroness's over-the-top opulent bathtub, with bubbles floating around her, surrounded by a sea of pink bathroom décor, and she still thought returning to Australia was sensible.

There was so much she didn't understand. This place. This man…

Bryn. The man who'd awakened a sliver of trust, who she'd thought…

Yeah, she wasn't going down that path.

She sank further into the bubbles and thought of what she'd seen so far. The dower house was a manor in miniature and it was pink as far as the eye could see. Pink carpets, pink settees, great bowls of fresh flowers, mostly pink. Chandeliers, glittering, reflecting the pink.

There were pink cupids on the ceiling she was gazing up at.

It should be enough to make the interior designer part of her bolt in horror, but it was so over the top it was fabulous. It was a fine line to admire such over-the-top pinkness, Charlie thought, and she wasn't sure whether she was brave enough to cross it.

She wasn't sure she was brave enough…for anything.

Where was Bryn now?

In the Hall? Surrounded by servants? Preparing luxury dog kennels for seven soon-to-be indulged dogs?

That was a crazy thought. It should make her smile but she didn't feel like smiling. She was so far out of her depth.

And he'd been angry. Was he still angry?

Forget it. Just do what comes next, she told herself, swiping bubbles from her nose. A week here max, to see the dogs settled, then home.

Where was home?

Oh, for heaven's sake… She had friends. She planned to couch surf while she found a paying job. She had clients who'd surely…possibly… return to her?

But first she had to get away from here.

Get away from Bryn?

'Don't think about Bryn,' she said out loud, but the words seemed to mock her.

Bryn Morgan.

Lord Carlisle.

She did need to go home.

This wasn't what he'd planned. He'd got her here, he had her on his land—and she was staying with his mother.

How had that happened?

He was a baron. Didn't that give him any rights? In the olden days a Peer of the realm could surely insist his wench meekly came at his bidding.

His wench? The thought made him grimace. Charlie was anything but. She was her own woman, a woman he didn't know enough but wanted to know more.

Heaven knew he'd exposed enough of himself to her now.

He was sitting in the Hall's vast kitchen, eating eggs and bacon and fried bread straight from the pan, feeding the odd crust to the collie at his feet. His father had given him Sadie as a pup. Bryn had been fifteen. The now ancient dog was now lying over his feet, oozing devotion. She was normally a comfort, but he couldn't find comfort now.

He should have told Charlie.

If he had she would have rejected him sooner. And now…he'd let his anger hold sway and he knew he'd frightened her.

'Dammit, Sadie, what would you do next?' he demanded and Sadie wagged her tail and looked hopeful.

Have another rasher of bacon, her look implied, and Bryn sighed and obliged. And thought of Charlie.

Another rasher of bacon?

If only it were that easy.

CHAPTER EIGHT

WHAT FOLLOWED FOR Charlie were three days in a sort of limbo. She slept fitfully. She walked Alice's Labradors for miles, exploring a countryside so different from the one she'd come from.

'There's an old copper mine with uncapped shafts on the western boundary,' Alice warned. 'The rest of the property's yours to roam, though. Neighbouring farmers are all Bryn's tenants, so tell them you're our guest and you'll be made welcome.'

She didn't tell anyone anything. She avoided everyone. As much as she could without appearing rude she even avoided Alice. Alice was friendly, open, aching to talk, but Charlie didn't want to talk.

She especially didn't want to talk to Bryn—and he didn't seem to want to talk to her.

Each morning he turned up to his mother's kitchen for breakfast in what seemed to be a long-standing tradition and he was…nice to her. But he was respectful of her boundaries.

She tried to respect his. She was here to settle

her dogs and her cows, and then she'd go home. She shouldn't ask questions.

But three days was a long time to hold back questions.

'Why don't you live in the Hall?' she finally asked Alice. Yes, she was being careful of boundaries but surely it wouldn't hurt to ask.

'Bryn doesn't like pink,' Alice said darkly.

Bryn had just left, striding off to do whatever peers of the realm did all day. Charlie was watching him as he negotiated the path through his mother's overcrowded—and very pink—rose garden and thought he looked anything but a peer of the realm. He looked like a farmer, in faded, stained moleskins, a khaki shirt with sleeves rolled to show muscled arms, his hair already tousled from working before breakfast, doing... what she was trying not to think he was doing. Being an ordinary farmer?

He wasn't. He was something that scared her.

'It wasn't just my love of pink,' Alice said and Charlie realised she'd been silent too long after her question and Alice had been watching her watching Bryn. Maybe she hadn't closed her face enough. Maybe something of what she was feeling was showing.

Except she didn't actually know what she was feeling.

'Sorry?' she said, feeling confused, and Alice

poured herself another cup of tea from a pot with pink roses all over it and prepared to expand. But with another cautious look at Charlie. It was as if she was measuring what she wanted to say against what she saw on Charlie's face.

'After the tragedy I was…in trouble,' she said softly. 'And so was Bryn. We'd lost so much. My father-in-law, brother-in-law and nephew had been living in the big house and we'd been living here, so suddenly there were two houses between three people. Bryn came home from university and threw himself into the breeding program. I grieved and did hardly anything but eventually I thought I'd redecorate. In pink.'

'Pink,' Charlie said faintly.

'I know it's over the top but I was desperate for a project,' Alice admitted. 'And I may have lost a little perspective. In the end Bryn said it was either pink or him, but, to be honest, we were both so grief stricken we were feeding each other. Seeing Bryn's grief made me sad and vice versa. Meanwhile Bryn's grandfather was like a ghost in that mausoleum of the Hall. It was the same between us. My father-in-law could hardly bear to look at me and I was no help to either of them. So Bryn moved over there. I knew it was awful. It was as if he was abandoning any chance he had of ever forgetting, of ever having fun, but there seemed no choice. He's done everything in his power to help his grandfather and I love him for it but I regret so much...'

Her voice trailed off. Bryn was striding into the distance with his ancient collie by his side. Charlie watched him go and thought of him as a teenager, hauled shockingly from university, trying to cope with his mother's and his grandfather's grief as well as his own.

'He's gone for the morning and then he's off to collect the dogs,' Alice said and Charlie realised that she was being watched. Alice was back to being brisk, practical and bossy. 'So now...wouldn't you like to see the Hall? You're an interior decorator and I'd love your opinion. Sooner or later Bryn will to have to put resources into the Hall, and, I'll admit, pink may not be the way to go. Though it's tempting. Come and tell me what you think.'

She hadn't been in the Hall. She didn't want to. She was almost...afraid to?

It was Bryn's home and there seemed all sorts of reasons she should stay away. The agreement was that she'd see the dogs settled and then she'd leave—without getting any more involved than she was now.

But Alice was rising, taking dishes to the sink, brisk and efficient.

'It's nonsense that you leave without seeing the Hall,' she told her. 'Two minutes while I redo my lipstick and let's go.'

* * *

So like it or not, she got the grand tour of the Hall, and at the end of it she was starting to see why Alice was veering towards pink. A one-solution-fitted-all approach seemed the only way to go when the prospect was so daunting. It was a vast mausoleum of a place, a three-storey rabbit warren with almost three hundred years of history.

Most of the rooms were dust-sheeted. 'We've never been brave enough to do more than peek under them,' Alice told her and Charlie peeked and saw a household frozen in time. Faded grandeur, mouse-chewed furnishings, great windows with massive, frayed drapes rotted with years of too much sunlight from the south-facing windows, or mould on the north-window drapes. There was one massive bedroom that looked ready to sleep in—the bed was made up and a fire laid in the grate, but it seemed that wasn't used either.

'That's where Bryn's grandfather slept,' Alice told her. 'When Bryn inherited the title I told him he should take it over. It's where every baron has slept since the Hall was built and I keep it ready. He has to accept it one day, but the idea of taking on that role… Alone…' She shook her head as if shaking off a weight and then kept going, towing Charlie from room to room until she felt her head spinning.

'This is crazy. How many bedrooms?'

'Fifteen,' Alice told her. 'Though I may have miscounted. The servants' rooms make it more. They're upstairs and horrid. I'd never put a servant in there. Not that we have servants any more. We have a lovely lady from the village who comes and cleans but Bryn said live-in servants make him nervous. We do have staff working with us on the land, of course. But come and see the living rooms.'

Living rooms! They were faded, ancient, never stepped in. Vast reception rooms, a ballroom, a great hall set up as a massive dining room, a library to take her breath away… This was true aristocracy stuff.

She was right to run, Charlie thought, as she wandered from room to room. That Bryn could possibly want her to stay…share…

The thought was crazy.

And then Alice led her into the kitchen and that gave her pause.

The kitchen was also vast but it was a used room. An enormous Aga took pride of place, radiating gentle heat. The floor was stone, worn with generations of use. The ceiling had wooden beams that seemed to match the enormous table running almost the length of the room.

Bryn obviously used this as his office and his living room. A computer sat at one end of the table, with a pile of bookwork. More bookwork lay on a beautiful old desk beside the dresser. A worn dog bed lay before the fire and the south sunlight shimmered through casement windows that looked feet deep. There was an ancient club lounge to one side, liberally covered with dog hair, and a small television on the top of the dresser. It was warm, comforting…great.

The place reeked of history, of centuries of good food and friendship, of warmth, of laughter…

Of home?

'We should put a false floor over these horrid stones,' Alice said. 'Linoleum would be so much easier on the feet.'

'Did she tell you she brought home samples of floor coverings?' And Bryn was there, standing in the doorway, smiling at his mother with fondness as well as exasperation. Seemingly unaware that Charlie had stilled in shock. 'And they were all…well, guess.'

Guess? When her heart was hammering in her chest? But some things were too obvious for words.

'Pink?' she managed, and there was that smile again…

'So, Charlie, what would you do with my kitchen?' he demanded, smiling straight at her. 'You're an interior designer. Pink linoleum?'

She had to collect herself. She had to ignore that smile and make herself breathe. 'Sorry, Alice, it'd be a crime,' she managed and she even managed to smile back at Bryn. 'The floor has to stay as it is. Most of this kitchen has to stay as it is. It's fabulous.'

'One in the eye to you, Mum,' Bryn said cheerfully and then he paused. 'Most?' he queried.

'I'd be tempted to sand back those beams,' she told him. 'You don't want to lose that fabulous patina of age but they were obviously put up rough. To be honest…a few hundred years of grease and spider webs… It could be improved.'

Bryn gazed up at the beams towering above their heads. 'I've never really looked,' he said thoughtfully. 'Spiders, eh? You'd destroy a three-hundred-year-old ecosystem just to make the place look pretty?'

'This place isn't meant to be pretty,' she retorted. 'But if you mean would I consider stopping the result of three hundred years of spider-breeding falling into my porridge, yes, I would.'

'We could lime-wash them pink,' Alice said happily and then as both Bryn and Charlie turned to look at her she giggled and held up her hands in surrender. 'I know. I'm letting go of my pink… slowly. It was there when I needed it but I'm moving on. Bryn, I haven't shown her the cellars or the outhouses yet but I'll leave them to you. Or your bedroom! He sleeps where the butler's supposed to sleep,' she told Charlie. 'Honestly, you can see what I'm up against.' She smiled at Charlie, a warm, deep smile that had meaning behind it, a meaning Charlie couldn't quite fathom—or didn't want to fathom. 'Meanwhile I have roses to deadhead. Bryn, I leave her to you.'

She bustled to the door, and then she paused and skewered her son with a look that mothers used the world over. Mostly parents used that look when they'd reached last resort. 'Clean your room or else…'

This direction was simpler.

'Make her stay,' she said and then she was gone.

Make her stay.

It was as simple and as complicated as that, Bryn thought.

It had nearly killed him to leave her be for the last few days, to know she was so close and yet so far.

Why hadn't he told her the facts from the start?

Because it wouldn't have made a difference, he thought. Or maybe it would. Maybe it would have stopped her coming here in the first place.

She was here to provide for the security of her grandmother's animals. That was all. She'd make sure he'd do what he'd promised and then she'd leave.

To go home to what? Debts up to her ears? He didn't need to be told the chances of her accepting more help from him were zero.

And further contact? The chances of that were zero as well.

'You want a job as an interior designer?' he ventured. 'This place is at your disposal.'

'But you've apparently already knocked back your mother's very kind offer.'

'I did at that.' He tried to smile, to make her smile back. It didn't come off. 'Charlie, stay.'

She tilted her chin and met his gaze. 'Why would I?'

'Because I want you to.'

'I don't understand why you would.'

'I'm sure you do,' he said gently. 'But I think you're afraid.'

'I'm careful. I need to be.'

'Of course you are. So accept this as a working proposition. Stay with Mum—she'll love it. Then work your way through this mausoleum and figure how we can make it a paying proposition.'

'You want to make this place pay?'

'It's too big for one man,' he said. 'Even if that man finds a wife, has a family, ends up with a dozen kids and even more dogs. My thought is that we could make part of it a luxury farm retreat. It's big enough for guests to be completely separate. It could be…fun.'

'Fun…'

'For…both of us? I'm guessing that's what's been missing in your life for a long time, Charlie *bach*.'

He was watching her face, watching for a reaction, and a reaction wasn't coming. Her expression was closed, wary, as if waiting for a trap.

He'd been around creatures enough to know that coming closer would be a disaster. He had to stay back, even though that edge of anger was making its presence known again. Why couldn't she trust?

'Wouldn't it be fun, though?' he said. 'To rip off the dust sheets, to uncover history, to work out what we could keep, what guests could use, what we ourselves should treasure.'

'We…' She said it as a whisper and he heard the fear. What the…?

'Mum and I,' he said, trying not to snap, and then as the fear didn't fade he decided to say it straight out. He'd shut up once and it had backfired. He had to be honest.

'Charlie, I'm about to say it like it is,' he said and he dug his hands deep into the pockets. What he was about to say should be said with a woman in his arms, but if he tried that he knew she'd run. 'I think I'm in love with you. I think you're the woman I want to spend the rest of my life with but you're looking at me like I have a loaded gun and I don't get it.'

'I'm sorry,' she whispered. 'But…love? We've known each other for how long?'

'For little more than a month. So yes, it's crazy,

but you know what's even crazier? I felt this way from about two hours after I'd met you. So that's being honest, Charlie, and now I need you to be honest back. Is it possible that you feel the same way?'

'I can't!' She sounded panicked.

'You can't or you don't?'

'L-look at this place,' she stammered. 'You're a baron. Lord Carlisle of Ballystone Hall. You own everything as far as the eye can see. If we got together... Okay, if we married... Baroness Carlisle? Lady Carlisle? How ridiculous is that?'

'It's just a title.'

'Which you didn't tell me about. How could I ever...?'

'Trust me? You did when you thought I was just a farmer. That's all I am, Charlie. The rest is an accident of birth. If I was born with a gammy leg would you still trust me?'

'I...of course... I mean...'

'Then what's the difference? I was born into a family with a title.'

'You didn't tell me.'

'Because I was still struggling with it myself. I still am. But it's surface. Something I'm stuck with. I hate that you're judging me for it.'

Silence. The ancient grandfather clock in the corner started its sonorous boom. One, two...all the way to ten. While Charlie watched him.

Oh, for heaven's sake, he thought. The rile of anger grew. He was exposing all here, and did she even get how hard it was to say it? But maybe what he was feeling wasn't anger. Maybe it was pain. Whatever, the clock reached its tenth gong and he was done.

'I can't force trust,' he said, and he could hear his own frustration. 'And I won't force anything. All I'm saying is that there's work here for you. You could stay, draw up plans for the Hall, think about what you'd like to see done—I trust you, you see, not to lumber me with pink. And we could take our time to see how things progress. Maybe they will and maybe they won't but you could trust enough to give it a try.'

'Bryn...'

'I've said enough,' he said roughly, not bothering to disguise the anger now. He glanced—unnecessarily—at his watch. 'I need to go,' he said. 'I have things to do before I collect the dogs. Isn't it lucky there's no room in the car for you? You'd be stuck with me for hours. You and me and seven dogs. You never know what I'd try on.'

'I don't...not trust you.'

'That's a lie,' he said brusquely. 'No matter. I'll bring the dogs back here and I'll care for them. Because I said I would, Charlie. You believed me that far at least. The rest...it doesn't matter. Or it can't matter. Leave it.'

* * *

Except it did matter.

She felt about three inches tall. Or maybe not even that much.

She should be driving to the airport to collect her dogs. *Her dogs.* He was doing this for her. He'd gone to enormous trouble and expense. The least she could do was trust him.

The problem was, though, that she didn't trust herself.

He could have sent one of the men to collect them. There was a small army attached to this estate, mostly tenant farmers who helped out with Bryn's herd, but also a farm manager and extra hands at need. She'd walked the estate and talked to enough people to know the lines blurred, between tenant, boss, neighbour and…friend.

Bryn was admired. Loved even. His crazy mother was adored.

So why couldn't she throw her hat into the ring?

Because she was afraid?

Or…because there was no way a woman like her deserved a guy like him?

Was that the crux?

Left alone, she wandered through the vast rooms of the mansion and thought of what she could do if she was given free rein. The tiny upstairs servant quarters would make ideal bathrooms. The grand rooms below could incorporate discreet staircases. A couple of the rooms at the end were big enough to put in the tiny lifts she'd read about, so those rooms could be fitted for the elderly or those with a disability. Guests would flock to stay in such a home.

She looked out of the windows at the rolling hills, turning to mountains in the background. At the sleek cattle grazing in the morning sun. At the tiny historic village down the road, at the tenants' houses, beautifully maintained.

This place was fabulous.

Bryn was offering her a place here.

She had no right…

He wanted her.

But for how long?

'So take a risk,' she told herself. 'You can trust again.'

It didn't work like that, though. Trust had to come from the heart, and it didn't operate on command.

She took a last glance around at the fabulous Hall, at a project that could keep her happy for years. She thought of Bryn. He was a man who could keep her happy…for ever?

Or not.

She knew she was a coward. She couldn't help it though. She wanted…to keep her heart safe.

She was going home.

CHAPTER NINE

To say seven dogs were excited to arrive at Bal-lystone Hall was an understatement. They'd been crated separately for the flight, then confined in the car.

Bryn opened the rear doors and the dogs leapt out in one unruly heap. The doors of the dower house were flung open. Charlie stood there beside his mother—and then Charlie was suddenly no longer standing. She raced through the garden path as the dogs raced towards her. She held out her arms and then she was on the ground, buried by a mass of hysterical, barking, joyous fur.

How many women would do this? Bryn thought. She'd sacrificed her business to try and get her grandmother out of trouble. She'd refused to send the dogs—and the cows—to refuges where they'd almost certainly eventually be put down. She'd travelled half a world to see them safely settled—she'd even had to trust him.

He was figuring it out by now, just what a big deal trust was. He'd done a bit of…sleuthing? His lawyers had hired investigators to try and find

Thomas' whereabouts. It hadn't seemed too big a deal—hardly even intrusive—to have them check on the ex-husband of Charlotte Foster.

'The guy seems almost as big a slime ball as your uncle,' his lawyer had told him yesterday. 'He's currently got bankruptcy proceedings against him and there's a paternity suit in progress. It seems like your Charlotte's one of a line.'

Your Charlotte. He thought of those words now as he watched her tumble with the dogs, holding as many as she could, laughing...weeping?

Yeah, weeping but there wasn't a thing he could do about it because he wasn't allowed near.

Because she'd been taught not to trust by experts, and who was he to undo years of distrust?

If she could love...

She certainly could, he thought, watching the mass of dogs, the laughter, the tears, the flying fur. He felt anger, frustration...love.

'She had a shower this morning,' his mother said. 'What a waste.' She was walking down the path to join him, watching the tumbling mass in approval. The Ballystone dogs were watching on the sidelines. They were clearly ready to check these new arrivals but even they seemed to know that what was happening between Charlie and her dogs was special. 'Are you going to introduce us?'

He could do that, mostly because it didn't require him taking his eyes off the tumbling, hugging Charlie. It even gave him time out from the aching hunger around his heart.

'Possum's the fox terrier,' he told her. 'She's missing an ear and she minds. When you greet her she'll put up a paw as if to hide it. Like she's embarrassed. Fred's part basset, part who knows what? His name should be Hoover because that's what he does. Hoovers everything up on the understanding that if it's not edible he can bring it up later. Flossie's the white scraggy mutt—part poodle, part a million other varieties. She's the one I hit, but as far as we can tell she's suffering no long-term consequences. The wolfhound's Caesar. He shakes when he's frightened and he's often frightened. Dottie's the Dalmatian. Her teats are hanging so low because she was used for puppy farming and then dumped when she'd outlived sequential pregnancies. Mothball's the Maltese fuzzball—you try and hurt Charlie—or even hug her—and you'll need to contend with Mothball. And finally there's Stretch… He's the one on top of Charlie now. A sausage dog. A vegetarian. He loves lentils but don't give them to him. His wind could clear the great hall.'

His voice trailed off. He was watching the mass of girl and dog.

His mother was watching him.

'You love her, don't you?' she whispered.

He didn't turn. The question hung.

'I was talking about the dogs,' he said at last.

'Surface talk,' she said dismissively. 'You love Charlie.'

'Yes,' he said simply because there was nothing else to say.

'But she's going home.'

He shrugged. 'Wherever home is. She has no money, no job, nothing. Here… I could offer…' He shrugged. 'It doesn't matter. She has to go her own way.'

'You could follow.'

'What, and leave you with the dogs?'

'For such a cause, yes. I'd even let them share my pink living room.'

'Greater love hath no parent,' he said and smiled and hugged her but his eyes were still on Charlie.

How could he make her trust?

He had no idea.

'Well, we're all eating in the great hall tonight,' Alice said, breezily cheerful again. 'We have seven new residents and we need to celebrate. Charlie, wiggle your way out of that tangle. Bryn, take the dogs and Charlie and show them their new home. I'm about to organise a feast.'

'Please, don't go to any trouble,' Charlie managed, emerging from dogs.

'No trouble at all,' Alice said, poking her son hard. 'It's Bryn who has to conquer…trouble?'

* * *

By dinner time the dogs were exhausted and happy to settle by the great fire in the massive dining room while their associated humans ate dinner.

Charlie was also exhausted but it wasn't physical exhaustion. Bryn had taken the dogs—and her—for a long exploratory walk over the estate. He'd been quiet for most of the time, peaceful even, strolling as if there were no undercurrents at all. He'd spoken only briefly, pointing out a cluster of heifer calves with obvious pride, showing her the field Cordelia and Violet would call home, showing her an ancient stone wall, which rumour had it had Roman foundations, talking of the problems with an old mining site on his west border and what the environmental people were doing now…

It was a gorgeous day and Bryn hadn't seemed to notice her silence. He'd simply been a good host, describing his land. He'd thrown sticks for the dogs, laughed at their antics. They were crazy happy to be out of confinement and he seemed content, too. He seemed…as if he was enjoying life.

For Charlie, though… Every moment brought a build-up of tension.

Why can't I relax? she asked herself. Why can't I just enjoy?

Why can't I treat this man simply as a friend?

Or more to the point… Why can't I let myself treat this man as more than a friend?

She was being stupid. A coward. She knew she was, but there wasn't a thing she could do about it. She'd dug her hands deep in her pockets and left them there, as if she suspected that if they escaped she might find her hand in Bryn's and how disastrous would that be?

Stupid, stupid, stupid, but by the time they'd walked the estate and she'd come home…no, not home…by the time they'd come back to the dower house…and Bryn had left her to clean up for dinner she was emotionally exhausted. Then, sitting at the vast dining-room table covered with peonies and sweet peas and roses, all in silver vases that must be worth a fortune, with the dogs by the fire, with Alice beaming and with Bryn watching her with that same gentle, understanding smile… By that time she was so tired she wanted to weep. Her defences were taking every ounce of self-control. The emotional barrier she'd built was impenetrable, to be defended at all times—but at what cost?

Alice had pulled in the big guns for the night. 'We do this for special,' she told Charlie happily. 'In the old days the family had chefs, undercooks, kitchen maids, butler, manservants, the works. Now I have a lady from the village and a couple of girls who pop in at need. I have no idea what all the servants did.'

'They catered to our every whim,' Bryn told her. 'But we can't think up enough whims to keep them employed.'

But Charlie wasn't thinking about whims. She was thinking of Alice's words. We do this for special. What was special about this night?

It was the night to mark…the end? The dogs were here and happy. She could go home.

The food, the setting, were magnificent. Charlie should have loved it. Instead she toyed with the food, trying to dredge up an appetite she'd completely lost.

The dogs seemed to be peaceful here already. Could she go home tomorrow?

'I enquired about flights while I was at the airport,' Bryn said, cutting across her thoughts. 'There are empty seats on a flight on Tuesday. Unless you want to stay until Cordelia and Violet…'

'I don't,' she said, too fast, and got a grave look for her pains. She caught herself. 'I'm sorry. That sounds…ungracious. But I do need to go home.'

'What will you do there?' Alice asked and Charlie thought Bryn wouldn't ask that. He'd guess how much it hurt.

'I have friends I can stay with until I find my feet,' she said, trying to sound more certain than she was. But she did have friends. She would be okay. 'There are always desperate calls for interior designers from socialites who want impressive party venues,' she told them. 'I have friends in the industry who'll give me casual work until I can organise myself again.'

'You'd rather organise parties than stay here and oversee the development of the Hall?' Alice asked in astonishment. 'I know...' She held up her hands to ward off Bryn's protest. He didn't want her pressured, but Alice had no such qualms. 'I understand Bryn not liking pink is an issue, but there are other colours.' She turned dreamy. 'Maybe we could have a marine theme. That might work being so far from the sea. A beachside holiday when there's no beach. A challenge... We could use something like Neptune's Retreat as the formal name and put Ballystone Hall in small letters underneath. We'd need to install a pool, though. With one of those wave makers?'

She was off and running and Charlie looked at Bryn and Bryn looked at Charlie and their lips twitched. More. There was laughter in both their eyes, but the laughter faded almost as soon as it appeared.

There was regret. Loss?

The home phone rang.

Saved by the bell, Charlie thought as Bryn

sighed and rose, but she didn't know what she was being saved from. Seeing the pain in Bryn's eyes? Reflecting her own pain?

'This is where we need a butler,' Bryn growled. The ladies who'd helped in the kitchen had gone home, so Lord Carlisle had to head out of the room and answer his own phone. He was trailed by all the dogs.

They heard him talking, briefly, urgently, and then he was back.

'The team reclaiming the mining site either didn't seal the fence properly when they left to-night or someone's been messing around up there looking at what they're doing,' he said brusquely. He looked only at Alice—as if Charlie were already gone? As if that final gaze had been a good-bye? 'Ewan Grady's cattle have broken through and so have some of ours. There are exposed shafts up there. We need to get them out before we lose any.'

'Ewan's one of our tenant farmers,' Alice told Charlie. 'I think I told you. The mine…they're uncapping the shafts to make more permanent repairs but at the moment they're exposed and dangerous. Bryn, do you want help?'

'Ewan and his son are there already,' Bryn told her. 'We don't want anyone up there who doesn't know the place backward.' And then finally he did look at Charlie. His face was grim. Because of his cows? Or because of her? 'Goodnight, Charlie,' he said brusquely. 'Sleep well.'

And he was gone.

Charlie was left looking at Alice. Who looked at her...with understanding.

Alice...

This woman had watched her husband leave to clean a water tank and he hadn't come back. And her daughter, too...

'He knows what he's doing,' Alice said soundly. 'Don't worry.'

'How can you ever stop worrying?'

'You have to trust,' Alice said gently. 'Otherwise you'll go mad.'

Alice started clearing but there wasn't much to clear. Charlie walked out to the massive front doors, opened them and watched the tail lights of the Land Rover. She watched them until they disappeared into the distance.

There was nothing she could do. She'd be no help up there.

If she stayed here...if she trusted...could she learn?

She closed her eyes and then Alice was there, touching her arm.

'Come and help me wash up,' she said gently. 'And don't look like that, sweetheart. Or if you do...think about what you can do about it.'

'I can't...'

'I think you probably can.'

She steered her back inside and closed the big doors after her. The dogs milled around their legs, excitement over. Heading back to the fire.

And Charlie stopped dead. Checked. Rechecked. And finally said it aloud.

'Alice…where's Flossie?'

Once upon a time Flossie's devotion had been absolute. That devotion had been repaid by dumping, by abandonment. Since then Flossie had learned new people, new devotion, but the last few days had been confusing to say the least. New country, new dogs, new faces…

Flossie had stood with the other dogs by Charlie's side but she'd seen tail lights retreating into the distance. She knew what that meant.

She'd started to run.

Alice and Charlie spent useless minutes searching the house, searching the yard, calling. 'She must have followed the car,' Charlie said at last. 'I had the door open. For a moment… I wasn't looking.' She felt dreadful but still…following the car would be okay. Surely? The mine wasn't so far that Flossie couldn't catch up, and the men would see her.

Bryn would rescue her yet again.

But she couldn't count on it. She wouldn't count on it.

'Can we go?' she asked, but Alice was already reaching for her jacket, grabbing a couple of pairs of wellies.

'Of course,' she said briskly. 'Bryn won't want Flossie up there while he's trying to herd the cows. Come on, sweetheart, let's go stop your dog being helpful.'

By the time Bryn reached the mine, Ewan and his son had already herded most of the cows to safety. A couple of younger cows were dodging them, though, maybe enjoying the excitement. Part of the fence was down, knocked by the cows?

Bryn turned to Ewan's son, a lad of about eighteen. 'Can you head back to the farm and get some decent rope so we can pull this fence back together?' Ewan's car was parked at the far side of the mine. 'Skirt right round,' Bryn said brusquely. 'No one falls down a shaft on my watch.'

He and Ewan returned to cornering, backing the two reluctant cows, working with torches, taking care at each step.

Flossie couldn't run as fast as the car but she kept it in her sights. By the time she reached the mine, though, the vehicle was parked, its lights off. There were men moving through the shadows with torches. There were cows.

This was unfamiliar. None of the voices seemed right.

And then, on the far side of the tailings, another vehicle… Tail lights.

It started steadily down the hill.

Flossie stared desperately across the tailings and knew what she had to do.

She didn't go around the tailings, though. She cut straight across. And halfway across…a shaft.

'What the hell…?'

The scream cut the night. It wasn't human, it was a high-pitched yelp, followed by the sound of shale falling. Something heavy falling with it.

A dog.

He and Ewan stilled and stared at each other.

'One of your dogs?' Ewan said, his eyes reflecting Bryn's horror. 'It must've followed…'

'Flossie,' Bryn said bleakly, instinctively guessing what had happened. They had the two young cows backed against the remainder of the fence. Their work was almost done. 'You get these two out and I'll check.'

He hardly needed to check, though. He picked his way carefully across the tailings, towards the shaft where the howl had come from.

He'd been through these tailings yesterday,

checking on the work, worrying about the open shafts and kids who wanted a bit of adventure. He'd rung the head of the team doing the work. 'I want those shafts covered, now.'

It hadn't happened.

The shaft where the noise had come from was probably the deepest.

Flossie…

Alice barrelled her beautiful sedan up the hill towards the tailings and Charlie was out of the door almost before the car stopped. Bryn's Land Rover was in front of them. A stout, squat figure Charlie didn't recognise was driving two cows forward. He made an urgent motion for them to stay back.

Charlie did as ordered, but it almost killed her to stay still while the cows were encouraged past the parked cars to join the herd further down the hill. Finally, with its members intact, the herd started moving placidly away. They were free to talk.

'This is Ewan,' Alice told Charlie. 'A neighbouring farmer. Ewan, have you seen…?'

'The dog? Is that what you're looking for?'

'Yes,' Charlie said thankfully. 'Is she here?'

'In a matter of speaking,' Ewan told her. 'There's a dog just fallen down a shaft. His Lordship's checking on her now. You ladies stay by the car. I need to find out what he's doing.'

* * *

Only of course they didn't stay by the car. Alice had torches in the trunk, a mother of a torch and a smaller one with a brilliant beam. 'We often find stock on the road,' Alice said, and the fluffy pink Baroness was suddenly a brisk and efficient farmer. 'We're used to dealing. Watch your feet, Charlie.' She tossed her a pair of wellies. 'You fall and Bryn will have my hide. You will not fall down a shaft.'

A shaft... Flossie...

Alice knew this land but was still ultra-cautious, picking her way between heaps of loose dirt. Charlie followed, feeling ill.

'They've made a right mess,' Alice said grimly over her shoulder. 'The shafts have been capped for over a hundred years. Our strategy was to fence it off more securely and reforest, until nature does the rest, but the conservation people said no, the capping has to be done properly. They've removed trees and dug out the old caps. Maybe they're right long term, but, oh, Charlie, some of these shafts…'

For the first time Charlie heard her voice falter. Alice had lost a husband and a daughter, Charlie thought. She was crossing loose tailings in the dark, heading towards her son who was…

Where?

Right over a shaft. Lying flat on his stomach so

he could point his torch down. For an awful moment Charlie thought he was lying on loose shale but then she saw he'd hauled timber up to make himself a solid base. There were lanterns set up beside him. Ewan and Bryn were both farmers. They'd be used to calvings at night, caring for stock. They were equipped, competent.

Safe? Not so much.

Bryn heard them come. He rolled sideways to talk as they approached. The ground was damp and mud had clung. He was filthy.

His face was grim under the dirt.

'She's down there. Hell, Charlie, I'm so sorry.'

That made her feel how small? Of all the things, that his first thought was to apologise to her…

'I let her out,' she told him. She was walking towards him but Alice clutched her arm and Ewan made an involuntary step to ward her off.

'Land's not stable any closer,' Ewan muttered, casting a worried look at Bryn. 'His Lordship shouldn't be there.'

But from below came a faint whimper, of fear and of pain.

Flossie…

'How…how deep?'

'Deep,' Bryn said grimly. 'But it goes deeper. She seems wedged on a ledge about twenty feet down. I can see her. She's lying still. If she moves, though…'

He stopped and Charlie saw a wash of anguish cross his face.

'I'll ring Davey and tell him to bring the gun.' It was Ewan, speaking softly but matter-of-factly behind them. He was a farmer, facing facts.

Dear God.

'Isn't there…? I could…' She wasn't even sure what she'd intended to say. Ring a rescue service, a fire department, what? If this were a child, maybe there'd be men and women prepared to risk their lives, she thought, but it *would* be risking lives. The shale was crumbly. These were ancient tailings and there'd been rain. Who knew what the state of the shaft would be?

A gun. A blast downward. A fast end.

Flossie.

The failures of the last few weeks—or maybe even the last years—were all around her. She'd brought the dogs over here. She'd set this tragedy up.

She couldn't help it. Her knees crumpled and she buckled and clutched her stomach.

'No gun,' Bryn snapped, cutting through her anguish. 'Charlie, don't look like that. I'm going down. Ewan, ring Davey and tell him to collect the climbing gear from the Hall. It's in the last stall of the stables. Tell him to wake John. He taught me to abseil as a lad. He's too old to do this now, but he'll make sure the gear's right and he'll supervise. Tell him to bring a couple more of the men. I'll need strength to haul us up. Mum, can you ring the Carlisle vet—have her on standby? Get her out here if she will. Charlie, there are planks over the pile of rubble near the Land Rover. Haul them over to make a solid base around the top of the shaft, working from where you are and slowly into me. We'll set up a line across the top of the shaft and rig torches facing down so I can see. Let's move, people. Go.'

'You can't!' She was aghast, but Bryn was already facing down again, assessing what he could see, focussing on what lay ahead. Alice stooped to kneel beside her, hugging her close, and she turned to her. 'Alice… Flossie…she's a dog. I can't ask…'

'You don't have to ask,' Alice told her.

Charlie thought wildly, this woman has lost so much, and here was her son, threatening to climb into an ancient shaft, threatening more grief? But…

'Bryn's not stupid,' Alice said and her voice was assured, with hardly a hint of the fear she must be feeling. 'He knows what he's doing, love,' she said. 'He wouldn't try this if he didn't think he'd succeed. I trust him and I think you should, too.'

Trust, Charlie thought wildly. How could she trust? He'd kill himself. Of all the—

'Charlie, don't make this a big deal.' Bryn's voice cut across her thoughts. He'd rolled again so he could face her across the tailings. 'I can see the sides of the shaft and they're looking stable. We can plank the top and run ropes from far back where we have solid ground. Flossie seems to have the sense not to struggle. If this was stupid I wouldn't be doing it. And Charlie...you might have let her out but this is not your call. Flossie officially belongs to me. She's my dog on my land. My decision. Tell her, Mum.'

And Alice even managed a smile. 'This is Bryn Morgan,' she said, a trace of laughter in her voice. 'He's Twelfth Baron Carlisle of Ballystone Hall, and what he says goes. We're mere minions, my dear. All we can do is trust.'

There was that word again. Was she kidding? Trust... How could she do that?

It seemed she had no choice.

Suddenly they had a team. Tenant farmers, workers at the Hall, the vet from the local village. They'd been summoned by Lord Carlisle but there was not a hint of resentment. Nor was there a murmur that what he was doing was stupid.

His lordship's dog was down the shaft. *His* dog. That was the story. Lord Carlisle was doing what he must to recover his own, and as Charlie worked she had a weird, almost ghostly sensation of centuries past, of the Barons Carlisle of Ballystone Hall through the ages expecting their wishes to be fulfilled.

There was respect here, though, and there was the trust that Bryn had asked from her. Respect and trust weren't things that could be inherited.

There was also concern. He was putting himself in harm's way and they cared.

As she cared?

How could anyone care as much as she did?

Bryn had given her a task and she was pathetically grateful. Instead of standing by, watching in fear, she was lugging timbers, working from far back, making the ground as stable as she could. As more people arrived they helped, and she was part of a team.

Bryn was organising ropes, working with Ewan and John. John was a grizzled guy in his seventies. She'd been introduced to him a couple of days earlier, Bryn's farm manager, a man of few words but reeking of common sense. His presence reassured her—a bit.

Not so much to stop the fear.

Alice was hauling timbers, too. They'd been dressed for dinner. Charlie had been wearing soft grey trousers and a turquoise blouse. Alice had been wearing a pale pink dress, beautifully tailored.

They were both now wearing a liberal coating

of mud. Neither of them cared. They were working side by side, grimly intent and Charlie knew that, despite her reassuring façade, Alice's fear was the same as hers.

Halfway through manoeuvring a plank into place she felt the fear hit in full force, a fear so great it immobilised her. She closed her eyes and went to say something, but Alice was beside her, firm and sure. Guessing what she was about to say out loud.

'Don't say it,' she said urgently. 'He won't listen.' And then, softly, speaking only to her, 'Charlie, this isn't all about the dog. He needs to get Flossie out of this shaft for himself. And for me.' She hesitated a moment and then added. 'And for you.'

'Alice, he can't.'

'He has to,' Alice said grimly. 'Ever since the tragedy… He blames himself for that day. He'd bought the petrol pump and shown his dad how to use it. He never…we never dreamed his father would use it underground.' She shook her head, as if shaking off a nightmare. 'Enough. That's past but now… Bryn struggles. He needs to learn to trust himself again.'

Bryn? Needing trust? The concept felt like turning the world on its head. She pushed it back, focussing on the closer thought. 'How can you bear it?' she whispered. 'If you lose him…'

'I won't lose him,' Alice retorted. And suddenly the grip on her shoulders tightened. 'But you... will you lose him? He's yours if you want him, Charlie Foster, but it takes courage.' She hesitated and glanced over to where Bryn was edging towards the shaft. 'It takes trust from both of you. Over and over again. You love and you love and you love and...'

Enough. Her voice broke. She let Charlie go and swiped angry tears from her face. 'You just do,' she said. 'Bryn's trusting us to keep this ground stable so are we going to stay here quibbling or are we going to cart more timber?'

And there was only one response.

They carted more timber.

Was he a complete idiot, risking his life for a dog?

This wasn't a dog, though. This was Flossie. Charlie's dog.

Would he do it for his own?

Yes, he would, he conceded, as he tightened his harness, letting John check and recheck. He'd do it because he loved Sadie. And his mother's dogs? Okay, they were useless but he loved them, too. And come to think of it...unless a dog was a stray...but then even if it was a stray... Could he point a gun when there was a real possibility of rescue?

He couldn't and that was something to remember. It was something to focus on other than the vision of the gaping shaft, the crumbling walls, oozing water, totally unstable.

They were rigging a rope ladder so he had something to keep his feet on, because finding footholds in shale walls reeked of stupidity and he wasn't stupid. Or not completely stupid. The plan was for two groups to lower him, one group controlling the ladder, the other the harness.

Every movement he made would be controlled from above. All he could do was trust. But these were people he'd known all his life. His mother. His people.

Charlie?

He glanced across at her anguished face. For a moment, their gazes met and held.

Locked.

A silent promise.

'I will come back to you,' his gaze said and he was sure she got it. And his next thought was an almost a primeval response to her look of anguish. 'I will come back and claim.'

How feudal was that? Feudal and sexist and totally inappropriate, he thought. Just lucky he didn't say it out loud. But then… Had she sensed what he was thinking? The way her lips curved… Was that a smile?

Maybe he wouldn't have to claim his feudal

rights, he thought. Maybe the maiden would come willingly.

It was a good thought. No, it was a great thought, inappropriate or not. It was a thought to carry him over the lip of the shaft and into the blackness of the void below.

It was the longest wait of Charlie's life. The team holding the ropes worked by inches. They were acutely aware of the crumbling structure of the shaft, that one false move, one solid bump if Bryn swung and hit the sides, could cave the whole thing in. They worked in almost total silence. Apart from the curt orders of the two in charge of ladder and harness, and the muffled words from the man being lowered, there was nothing.

They were dropping the ladder, the harness, the man, in measured steps. The two in charge set a beat to work to. One, two, down, one, two, down. Every downbeat meant the ropes were eked out a couple of inches at a time.

It was infinitely, agonisingly slow. For those in the background it was killingly slow.

Charlie was clutching Alice and Alice was clutching Charlie. Who knew what Alice was thinking? All Charlie knew was that they were almost conjoined, linked by their love of the man being lowered down the shaft.

Love. There was a huge concept.

Or maybe it wasn't. How many songs were there in the world about love? How many forms did love take?

The first flurry of romantic love? The hormonal rush that blinded to a lover's flaws? The love she'd thought she'd had for the man she'd once so disastrously married?

Or this, she thought, the idea embedding and growing as time stretched on? A love that was deep and abiding. A love that transcended romantic.

A love that said trust was bone deep.

She stood and watched Ewan, lying at the top of the shaft, pointing his torch downward, directing operations. Both teams were well back, lowering their ropes secured with planking. Only the ropes inching downward denoted anything was below.

Her whole world was below. It was a man descending into the blackness to save a dog that, whatever he said, wasn't his. Flossie was her dog.

But it didn't matter. She knew at some deep, instinctive level that he'd be doing the same if it weren't her dog. She looked at the people around her, the tenant farmers, the workers from the Hall, even his mother, and she saw fear but she also saw total trust.

This man was…their man. Their trust and their love was absolute.

And what she was feeling right now bought into that. It was nothing to do with fear, she thought. It was so much more. It was as if something had washed through and left her completely, irreversibly changed.

'Bryn,' she whispered and it was so much more than a word.

It was a vow.

And then there was a sharp, muffled command from below. Both teams stilled and the whole world seemed to hold its breath. The silence went on and on. No one moved. No one spoke.

And then, finally...

'Up.' The single syllable was almost a grunt, as if a truly Herculean effort was being made. It was enough to start the teams again. Once again though, they worked with agonising slowness. There was just as much risk raising as in lowering, maybe more, because if he was carrying Flossie there'd be more weight.

She didn't know if he was carrying Flossie. The teams would know because of the change in weight but Bryn was wasting no words, no effort, in reporting.

And Charlie wasn't asking. She was no longer thinking of Flossie.

Bryn. Her love. Her man.

And finally he was nearing the top. There were curt orders from Ewan, because he still wasn't safe. Dragging him over the edge could make things collapse. But Ewan and John were lying full length on the planking, grasping with a strength she couldn't imagine. A limp bundle of fur was being passed up, seized, dragged backward.

She should rush forward. Flossie was her dog. Flossie was what this was all about. But other hands were taking Flossie. The vet was here, giving orders, carrying Flossie away from the shaft so she could see the damage.

But Charlie's gaze was still locked on the shaft. On Bryn. On the final few inches.

He was being hauled upward, his arms grabbed, tugged backward to safety. He was standing. John and Ewan were half holding, half hugging, their grimed faces a mix of triumph and relief.

He was safe. He was standing on firm ground, looking around. Seeing his mother, giving her a faint smile. And then…seeing her.

Looking. Just looking.

And that look… The promise in that gaze… With it, the loneliness and distrust inside her cracked and then shattered—and then disappeared as if it had never been.

She smiled. It was a crazy, tear-filled smile, a smile she'd never known she possessed but it was his, all his.

And finally she walked forward, through the

mud, across the planking, to take the man she loved into her arms.

It was the moment when Charlie Foster gave her heart for ever.

Flossie was headed for a night at the veterinary clinic. It was miraculous that she'd survived, but her injuries were a little more serious than when she'd had her encounter with the car. Her leg was broken this time, and she had myriad grazes. 'She'll be okay,' the vet told them. 'But a bit of sedation and some IV fluids will help her recover faster.'

They thanked everyone. Charlie hugged everyone. It was hard to hug when she was being hugged herself but from the moment he'd surfaced, Bryn had his arm around her. He seemed to need the contact.

That was fine by her. Contact... Body against body. Bryn.

He was by her side. He was safe.

Bryn.

Alice's sedan proved no match for mud stirred by the vehicles of those arriving to help. It had to be abandoned to be collected in the morning so they drove home together. They drove in near silence—the emotions they were all feeling left little room for words. Bryn pulled up outside the dower house, helped his mother from the car, hugged her hard and then turned to Charlie.

'There's room in my bed tonight,' he said simply and Alice smiled as if she'd expected those exact words. She kissed Charlie and then slipped through her front door and closed it behind her.

So Charlie came on home with him because... that was how it felt. Suddenly this vast mausoleum of a Hall was...home.

Because Bryn was there.

They showered, still almost in silence. Together. It felt right. It hardly even felt sexy. Bryn's body showed the marks of rope burn, scratches where Flossie had struggled, grazes. Charlie helped him clean them, loving every mark.

'Love,' Bryn said softly as the final graze gave up its mud. And he tugged her into his arms, snagged towels and carried her up the grand staircase to the vast bedroom, to the four-poster bed that the Barons Carlisle of Ballystone Hall had slept in for generations.

'Because it's time we took our place where we belong,' he told her.

He lowered her onto the sheets and she smiled and smiled. And then she claimed her man.

Her man. That was what it felt like, she thought as she woke in the soft dawn light. She was spooned in his arms; the warmth enveloping her was something she'd never felt before...

'I'm in love,' she whispered into the dawn, and the arms holding her tightened.

'I hope so,' Bryn growled. 'If not we're in trouble because this is your home. Now and for ever.'

Now and for ever. She let the words drift.

They were just words.

They were the most important words she'd ever heard.

But some things had to be said. This man had done nothing but give, while she…

'Bryn, I didn't trust you,' she whispered. 'I'm so sorry.'

He turned her then, gently, so their faces were inches apart on the great down pillows. 'Life's taught you not to trust,' he told her.

'Life's kicked you around, too.' She hesitated but it had to be said. There was room for nothing but honesty now. 'And death. So much tragedy… how can you still love?'

'I was lucky,' he said simply. 'Those I loved gave me so much love in return.' He leaned forward that last couple of inches and kissed her, tenderly, with all the love in the world. 'You get love, you give love,' he said softly. 'It seems to me, Charlie *bach*, that it's been lacking in your life. There was only your grandparents to love you. Now though… You have seven dogs, and a couple of cows arriving some time soon. You have Alice, who's already crazy about you. And you have me. So that's, let me see, eleven known love donors. With that much love coming your way, my Charlie, do you have enough to send some back my way?'

And there was only one answer to that. She tugged him into her and kissed and then there was no room for words for a very long time.

They slept again and when they woke...

'I know I should do this properly,' Bryn said sleepily, holding her close. 'Fancy restaurant, orchestra, ring cunningly hidden in the chocolate soufflé...but if you feel we can get by without the soufflé... Charlie, will you marry me?'

Would she marry him? Would she wake beside him for the rest of their lives? Would she trust this man with her heart, with her love, with her future?

How could he ask such a question? The answer was all around them, an aura so strong surely he could see it. There was love in this room. Love and laughter and dogs and maybe kids and maybe even grandkids and wonder and hope and trials and joy.

Marriage... The joining together of two people who loved each other to the exclusion of all others.

Two people who trusted each other for life.

He was asking for an answer. He really didn't know? She saw the trace of uncertainty in his eyes, the trace of doubt behind his eyes and she couldn't bear it. She smiled and she smiled and her fingers touched his lips, his face. It was a battered face this morning, scratched and bruised.

She loved it. She loved him.

The question hung. Charlie, will you marry me?

'How can you doubt it?' she whispered. 'Bryn, you've trusted me from the start but me...it's taken me a while but I'm there now, with all my heart. Will I marry you? Yes, my love, I will.'

They loved again and then they slept, and woke when the sun was high and Alice was calling up the stairs.

'Hey, you two, don't you believe in answering the phone? I phoned the landline and your mobile phone. Nothing.'

'I turned my phone off,' Bryn whispered to Charlie. 'You want to pretend we're not here?'

There were dogs scratching at the door. Alice was still below stairs, obviously respecting their privacy—a bit—but by the sound of her voice she was full of import and Charlie wouldn't put it past her to power up the stairs and burst right in.

'My phone must have got wet down the shaft last night,' Bryn called out. 'Mum, can you take the dogs? Charlie and I are...busy.'

'Busy!'

'We're also engaged,' he called and Charlie almost choked at the thought of Alice's face downstairs. But it seemed Alice was made of too stern a stuff to be distracted by a little thing like an engagement.

'About time,' she retorted. 'But I have news.'

'News?'

'Thomas has been arrested in Thailand,' she told them. 'And we have an extradition treaty with Thailand. End of scams, Bryn. He's coming home to face trial.'

'Excellent,' Bryn murmured and Charlie heard a gasp of what was surely indignation from below stairs.

'Is that all you can say? Bryn, don't you care?'

'It's good that he's stopped from scamming,' Bryn said, tugging Charlie close again. 'But for the rest… Nope, don't care.'

'Bryn…'

'I have other things to care about than my sordid uncle,' Bryn said, smiling at Charlie. And such a smile… 'I have many things to care about, the loveliest being in my arms right now. So, Mum, if you don't mind…would you be good enough to take the dogs for a walk so I can get back to my caring?'

There was another gasp from downstairs and then a choke of laughter. But then…ever the mother. 'You're not holding her against her will, are you, Bryn? Charlie, are you okay?'

'I'm fine,' Charlie called back, choking on laughter. Choking on happiness. Choking on love. 'I'm absolutely fine.'

'We're both fine, Mum,' Bryn called. 'And we intend being fine for the rest of our lives so if it's okay with you…fine starts now.'

CHAPTER TEN

THE WEDDING OF Bryn Thomas Morgan, Twelfth Baron Carlisle of Ballystone Hall, was a great occasion, bruited not only in the neighbourhood but in the society pages across Britain. Since the tragedy, given the Eleventh Baron's age and distress, the media had left this family alone, but now they woke to the fact that one of its most eligible aristocrats was about to wed. Journalists and photographers thus descended as a pack, expecting…pomp?

They didn't get pomp.

By rights the wedding should have been held in the family chapel, or in the little village church, but this was a celebration the like of which the district hadn't seen…for ever? The shared joy of Flossie's rescue seemed to have embedded Charlie in the hearts of the district—they'd seen her lugging timber—they'd seen her distress and her joy at the happy ending. They'd also seen the way the Baron had come straight to her, the way he'd held her. This was a happy ending beyond happy endings. The joy between Charlotte Foster and

Lord Carlisle was thus deemed to be a fine thing and it was something to be shared.

The wedding was therefore held outside, on the lawns of Ballystone Hall. A massive marquee was set up—decorated mostly in pink because Alice was in charge of decorations and both Charlie and Bryn thought, Why not pink? They were so happy, why shouldn't Alice be, too? So as the music swelled, as the time approached, Bryn stood with John by his side, under an arch of pink roses.

Waiting for his bride.

But first came the dogs because the dogs had brought them together and dogs would be part of their lives for ever. There were ten dogs, each walked by their own attendant.

First, Bryn's Sadie walked by Ewan.

Then Alice's two dogs, walking on either side of Ewan's wife, the lady who *did* for Alice. Eilwen was beaming and beaming and it seemed almost as if the dogs were beaming as well.

And then came the Australian contingent. They were led by the six people who'd offered them forever homes, four tenant farmers, the local postmistress, and the head of the conservation team. He'd come to the Hall the day after the shaft drama with apologies and gone home with Stretch, the sausage dog. Stretch was now in charge of making shafts safe, or at least supervising the team doing it. For bureaucratic reasons the two dogs now living away from Ballystone were deemed borrowed, not given, but that was okay. It meant they still had to visit and all six dogs had owners who loved them.

Happy ending all round?

Absolutely, for here was another happy ending. Flossie was walking by herself. She was carrying a limp, but maybe a limp wasn't a bad price to pay for her happy ever after. For the Hall was her forever home now. They could leave the doors, the gates open all they wanted. There was no way she'd leave.

And Bryn had trained her for her role today. She was carrying a ring box around her neck. Flossie. Ring bearer.

She reached Bryn's side and sat as he'd taught her. He put a hand down to pat her head but Bryn wasn't looking at Flossie.

He was looking at his bride.

For Charlie was walking steadily towards him. Alice was by her side, her sole attendant, the woman she'd chosen to 'give her away'. Alice, beaming and beaming. In glorious pink.

But he wasn't looking at his mother, either.

He was looking at Charlie.

She was wearing a rainbow.

'You can wear white.' He'd heard Alice discussing it with her. 'Yes, it's your second marriage but no one cares. But I know where we can order you the most beautiful pink gown…'

He would have even married her in pink, he thought, the smile in his heart growing by the moment. But he didn't have to marry her in pink., because this was Charlie and Charlie had blossomed. Charlie had opened, unfurled, trusted and…loved. One colour would never be enough for this woman.

For Charlie was her own woman. She knew what she wanted. The dress she was wearing was simple but wonderful, a wafting creation of rainbow silk. It had tiny capped sleeves, caught in under her breast and then swirling out, a cloud of rainbow colour. She'd let her curls fall free. A cluster of rosebuds nestled in her curls and she was wearing diamond eardrops that had been in his family for generations.

'What if I lose them?' she'd protested.

'I'll buy you more,' he'd promised. 'But they're just things, Charlie *bach*. Lose them or not, it doesn't matter. All that matters is you.'

So she did wear them, because they fitted the outfit perfectly. They were just…what she wanted?

Except they weren't what she wanted. He knew that now. This was Charlie, and even if she'd worn nothing in her ears, it wouldn't have mattered. She wanted him.

And Bryn? He wanted Charlie, with all his heart. He wanted her smile. He wanted to wake every morning with her beside him. He wanted his Charlie to love him for ever, and magically she wanted it just as much as he did.

She was reaching him now, pausing for just a moment to pat Flossie because Flossie was being extraordinarily good and a woman had to give a dog her due. But her smile didn't leave Bryn.

'Hey,' she whispered and they might as well have been alone.

'Hey, yourself,' he whispered back and it was too much. She was so achingly beautiful. Before the crowd, before all these people, he lifted her and swirled her so her dress flared out in a riotous circle of colour. The guests and the media went wild. Then he used the time while the vicar waited for the crowd to settle to kiss her as he needed to kiss her. As he intended to kiss—and be kissed—for the rest of his life.

'Hey,' he said again, as finally they broke apart, as finally reality broke in. 'You want to get married?'

And she looked up at him, mistily, through tears, this man she loved with all her heart. This man she'd trust for ever. This man... Her man.

'I think I already am married,' she whispered

back and finally they turned to face the patiently waiting vicar. 'That's the way I feel. But let's say I do.'

So they did.

For the rest of their lives.

* * * * *

*If you enjoyed this story,
check out these other great reads
from Marion Lennox*

The Billionaire's Christmas Baby
Stranded with the Secret Billionaire
Stepping into the Prince's World
His Cinderella Heiress

All available now!